HEART
OF A
CHAMPION

ELLEN SCHWARTZ

TUNDRA BOOKS

Tundra Books, a division of Random House of Canada Limited, a Penguin
Random House Company

Library and Archives Canada Cataloguing in Publication

Schwartz, Ellen, 1949–, author
      Heart of a champion / Ellen Schwartz.

Issued in print and electronic formats.
ISBN 978-1-77049-880-8 (bound).–ISBN 978-1-77049-882-2 (epub)

      I. Title.

PS8587.C578H33 2016   jC813'.54   C2015-901052-7
                                                 C2015-901053-5

Published simultaneously in the United States of America by Tundra Books of
Northern New York, a division of Random House of Canada Limited, a Penguin
Random House Company

Library of Congress Control Number: 2015931504

Edited by Sue Tate
Designed by Rachel Cooper
The text was set in Garamond
Printed and bound in the United States of America

Tundra Books,
a division of Random House of Canada Limited,
a Penguin Random House Company
www.penguinrandomhouse.ca

1   2   3   4   5   20   19   18   17   16

Penguin
Random
House
TUNDRA BOOKS

For the "out-laws" Margo, Alan, Bill and Julie

FOREWORD

Heart of a Champion is a delightful story that captures the essence of the Japanese spirit through the lives of children. The author, Ellen Schwartz, has thoroughly researched the times by talking extensively with members of the Japanese Canadian community. She met Kaye Kaminishi, our last surviving Asahi baseball player, who was a rookie in 1941, and sought out the facts by conducting interviews, reading books and watching films. The story has surprising elements of reality, from the food eaten to the description of events following the bombing of Pearl Harbor.

More than one hundred years after the founding of the Asahi club, the publication of this book is a fine tribute to the players, who were revered like movie stars. To many young boys of the prewar era living on Powell Street and all over British Columbia, being an Asahi baseball player was the ultimate goal. Fathers of the players were proud and supported the many levels of clubs that fed into the team. Asahi players were treated to food and drink after the games and did not have to pay for an *ofuro* (soak in a Japanese bath). The Asahis not only bridged the gap between the Caucasians and the Japanese who shared a community, but also the generation gap between the first and second generation Japanese Canadians. The story of the Asahis is a story of triumph over adversity and pays tribute to a group of Japanese Canadians who found a way to excel. In 2003, the team was inducted into the Canadian Baseball Hall of Fame, and, in 2008, was designated an Event of National Historic Significance.

Heart of a Champion is a heartwarming story of friendship and love through challenging times.

Linda Kawamoto Reid
Research Archivist, Nikkei National Museum,
Burnaby, British Columbia

ACKNOWLEDGMENTS

The author is grateful for the assistance of The Canada Council for the Arts in their support of this project.

 Canada Council   Conseil des arts
for the Arts   du Canada

For their generous offer of a writing space: James and Lynn Hill.

For their helpful comments in reading the manuscript: Graham Bibby, Heather Duff, Morna McLeod, Chris Petty, Aaron Rabinowitz, Linda Kawamoto Reid, Bernard Rosenberg, Bill Schwartz, Merri Schwartz, Lori Thicke, Yukiko Tosa and Irene Watts.

For their invaluable assistance in arranging interviews and providing historical information: Richard Hambly, Sakaye Hashimoto, Noboru Hayashi, Momoko Ito and the staff of the Nikkei Internment Memorial Centre, Jean

Kamimura, Kaye Kaminishi, Marion Lesnik, Linda Kawamoto Reid and the staff of the Nikkei National Museum & Cultural Centre, members of the Tashme Historical Project (Tak Negoro, Shoji Nishihata, Linda Kawamoto Reid, Howard Shimokura, Kaz Takahashi and Jean Wakahara), Grace Eiko Thompson, Yukiko Tosa, Irene Tsuyuki and Barbara Yeomans.

AUTHOR'S NOTE

Several years ago, I saw a documentary on television about the Vancouver Asahi baseball club. I was dazzled by the skill, professionalism and dignity of the team. When the film was over, I said to myself, "Why have I never heard of the Asahis before? They were amazing! Every Canadian kid should know about them!" So, because I write books for children, I decided to write one about the Asahis.

Americans introduced baseball to Japan in the 1870s, and it didn't take long for the Japanese to excel at the game. When Japanese immigrants started arriving in Canada in the early 1900s to work as fishers, loggers and laborers, they formed baseball teams in their new home. In 1914, a group of players, under the leadership of Coach Matsujiro "Harry" Miyasaki, formed the Vancouver Asahi baseball club. *Asahi* means *morning sun*, so perhaps the name reminded the players of their homeland in the Far East.

As Japanese, they were smaller than their white opponents. They didn't have the size and strength to hit home runs. They had to outthink and outrun the competition rather than out-slug them. So they developed a style of baseball called smart ball, or brain ball, relying on bunting and stealing bases to win games.

It worked. The Asahis soon dominated baseball in Vancouver, winning their first title, the Vancouver International League championship, in 1919. The team went on to win many more championships in the years that followed, defeating both Japanese and white teams throughout the Pacific Northwest.

This was at a time when Asian Canadians were considered second-class citizens. They were not allowed to vote, had to sit upstairs in theaters and were denied many types of jobs. Some white players and fans resented the fact that a Japanese team was beating them at their own game. The Asahis suffered racial slurs and even attacks on the field. But they kept their discipline and their dignity. By following a code that emphasized teamwork, hard work and fair play, they became a symbol of pride in the Japanese community. As one fan, Frank Moritsugu, said, "They made it possible for the rest of us . . . to hold our heads higher."

Slowly the Asahis won over white fans, too. By the late 1930s and early 1940s, both Japanese and white fans thronged the Powell Street Grounds and cheered them on as they won five Pacific Northwest League championships in a row, from 1937 through 1941.

When the Asahis celebrated their victory in September 1941, they could not have known that it would be their last.

In 1939, Germany invaded Poland, and World War II began. France and Great Britain declared war on Germany, and Canada, as part of the British Empire, joined the war on the British side.

Over the next two years, while the war raged in Europe, Japan was moving across Asia, overrunning parts of China, the Soviet Union, Mongolia and Indochina. On December 7, 1941, the Japanese navy attacked a United States naval base at Pearl Harbor in Hawaii. At the same time, Japan declared war on the United Kingdom, Canada and the United States.

In Canada, Japanese Canadians were branded "enemy aliens" and quickly lost their rights. The government, fearful that they would be loyal to Japan and would share war secrets with the enemy, took away their fishing boats, cars, radios and cameras. The Japanese were subject to a dawn-to-dusk curfew.

In the spring of 1942, the Canadian government began to remove Japanese Canadians from the west coast of British Columbia. Men between the ages of eighteen and forty-five were sent to road camps in the interior to build roads. Women, children and older people were sent to internment camps, many in abandoned mining or logging "ghost towns." Small, primitive shacks were hastily built to house them. The people lost their homes, businesses and possessions, never to get them back.

The removal of the Japanese from the coast spelled the end of the Vancouver Asahi baseball club. Players were dispersed to different internment camps, and people were too worried about surviving, at first, to think about baseball. But the Asahi players had taken the spirit of baseball with them. They formed teams in their camps and competed against squads from other camps and nearby towns. The crack of the bat rang out, cheering the residents of the camps.

Although World War II ended in 1945, the Canadian government did not allow Japanese Canadians to return to the west coast until 1949. Most had lost their homes and possessions. They had to build their lives all over again.

In 1988, the Government of Canada formally apologized to Japanese Canadians for their treatment during

World War II. In 2003, the Vancouver Asahi baseball club was inducted into the Canadian Baseball Hall of Fame. Two years later, they were named to the British Columbia Sports Hall of Fame.

HEART

OF A

CHAMPION

1

Kenny Sakamoto raised his head from the pillow. Across the room, his older brother, Mickey, was fast asleep, his chest gently rising and falling. Kenny hadn't even heard Mickey come in the night before; he and his teammates must have been out late, celebrating.

Kenny tiptoed out of the room. The house was quiet. The door to Mom and Dad's room was still closed, and so was that of his little sister, Sally. Kenny fetched the newspaper from the front step and opened it at the kitchen table.

Holy smokes! Today, September 2, 1941, baseball had the top headline. It even came before news of the war!

VANCOUVER ASAHIS MAKE IT FIVE
CHAMPIONSHIPS IN A ROW!
16-YEAR-OLD MITSUO "MICKEY" SAKAMOTO SLUGS
DOUBLE TO CLINCH NINTH-INNING VICTORY

And there, just below the headline, was a picture of Mickey the moment after making that glorious hit, his upper body twisted, the bat flung out from his left hand. In the background, the ball sailed toward left field, the runners on second base and third base were poised to start dashing, and the arms of the Asahi fans were raised in the air.

Staring at the photo, Kenny felt himself transported back to yesterday's Pacific Northwest League championship game.

The Powell Street Grounds stands had been packed, people standing elbow to elbow, everyone wearing their white Asahi caps emblazoned with the red *A*. Kenny was crushed between Dad and Mom. On the other side of Mom, Sally bounced up and down on her seat like a jack-in-the-box.

The cheers of "Go, Asahis!" and "Yay, team!" faded to a nervous silence in the top of the ninth inning when the opposing team, from Fife, Washington, pulled ahead. *This can't be happening*, Kenny thought. *The Asahis—pride of the Japanese community, winners of four straight Pacific Northwest League titles—can't be losing!*

In the bottom of the ninth, the first Asahi player bunted. The second player singled. Both stole bases to advance to third and second. "That's the way, boys! Now we've got it!" people shouted.

The next player struck out. The next flied out.

A groan escaped from the crowd.

Mickey came up to bat.

He's only a rookie, Kenny thought. *Two out and the game on the line—it's too much pressure.*

Kenny's heart started beating fast. *Calm down*, he told himself. *Don't get overexcited*. He couldn't help it. He could barely look.

And then—the crack of the bat. The arc of the ball. The runner on third base reached home. The runner on second rounded third. Mickey raced past first. The second runner scored the go-ahead run just as Mickey slid into second. Safe!

The Asahi players mobbed Mickey, pounding him on the back. The stands erupted. People threw their Asahi caps into the air. "Victory!" they chanted. "Hurrah, Asahis! Hurrah, Sakamoto!" Mom broke into a wide grin. Sally jumped to her feet, shouting, "That's my brother! That's my brother!" Dad stood tall, looking down at the field. His face was solemn, but Kenny could see a sheen of tears in his eyes as he beamed straight at his son. The hero.

———

Now, Kenny came back to himself, to the kitchen, to the newspaper spread out before him. After describing the Asahis' come-from-behind victory, the article recounted the glorious history of the baseball team, the hundreds of wins since its founding in 1914, the tradition of outstanding bunting and base running, and the code of dignity and discipline on and off the field. Kenny knew all this already, but he read it through anyway, savoring every word.

And then he saw it. Just below the article, there was a small advertisement.

CALLING ALL BOYS! TRYOUTS FOR ASAHIS
AND JUNIOR TEAMS IN SPRING 1942

SHIGUN *(Clovers)* – AGES 9 TO 11

SANGUN *(Beavers)* – AGES 12 TO 14

NIGUN *(Athletics)* – AGES 14 TO 16

ASAHIS – AGES 16 TO 20+

MARCH 1942: DATES AND TIMES TO BE ANNOUNCED

Kenny stared at the notice.

Could I? I'm nine now. Old enough for the Clovers.

No. Impossible. Mom and Dad would never let me.

Is there a way . . . ?

No. Forget it. I'm no good at baseball. Besides, I can't run to save my life.

But if only . . .

Kenny fetched a pair of scissors and clipped out the ad anyway. But now there was a hole in the newspaper, and Dad would wonder why. Kenny thought for a moment, then cut out the entire article about the Asahis, as if he had purposely clipped it for Dad. Maybe his father wouldn't notice that there was an extra bit missing.

Just as he thought this, footsteps padded down the hallway. Kenny looked for someplace to hide the notice. The pocket on the front of his pajama top! He stuffed it in. *Funny*, he thought, *that the pocket is right over my heart. If Dad knew I was even thinking about it . . .*

Dad, still unshaven, came to the kitchen table. "Morning, Kenny. You feeling okay?" he said automatically.

"Fine, Dad." His constant reassurance.

Dad patted his shoulder. When he saw the picture of Mickey, he broke into a smile. "Well, now," he said, scanning the article. He didn't say more, but his face lit up with quiet pride.

Without being asked, Kenny got Dad's scrapbook and pot of glue. He turned to the first empty page in the bulging book, past pictures of Mickey coming up from the Clovers, through the Beavers to the Athletics and finally to the Asahis—at sixteen, one of the youngest players ever to make the team. Past Mickey's rookie picture, his thick eyebrows raised in surprise, as if he couldn't believe he was an Asahi. Past newspaper reports on every game Mickey had played in.

After Kenny helped Dad paste the new article into the scrapbook, Dad turned to him. "Last day of summer vacation, eh, Kenny? What are you up to today?"

Kenny looked away. While he had been helping Dad, an idea had come to him. *I'll have to get Mickey alone, and I'll have to really sweet-talk him. And, of course, Mom and Dad can't know, or even suspect, a thing.*

"Oh, nothing much," he said, hoping he sounded normal. "Just play around the neighborhood, I guess."

"Don't overdo it, okay?"

Kenny stood up to put the glue away.

Did Dad notice I didn't answer?

Kenny hovered over his brother's bed. Mickey slept on, his black hair spiked on the pillow. His strong shoulders strained against his shirt; when Kenny looked closer, he saw that it was his Asahi uniform. He grinned. Mom would have a fit if she knew her son had slept in dirty, sweaty clothes, but Kenny didn't blame him. *If I had an Asahi uniform, I'd sleep in it, too*, he thought. Above Mickey's headboard, the wall was plastered with pictures of Asahi players. On Kenny's side of the room, too.

Mickey rolled over and stretched.

Kenny leaned in close. "Mickey, can I talk to you?"

"Oh, hi, Kenny." Mickey yawned. "Sure, what is it?"

Kenny's eyes darted sideways. Even though they were in their room, with the door closed, he didn't want to take any chances. "Not here. Outside."

"What's the big—"

"Shhh!"

Mickey looked perplexed. "Okay, just let me wash up." He headed toward the bathroom. Kenny followed him into the hall, but was stopped by Mom.

"You ready, Kenny?"

"For what?"

"Doctor's appointment, remember?"

"Aw, Mom, it's the last day of vacation."

She narrowed her eyes. "Kenji Sakamoto . . ."

Kenny knew he was in trouble when she used his Japanese name. He followed his mother to the front door and bent down to tie his shoes. "Will it take long? I have . . . uh . . . something I want to do with Mickey."

She looked at him sharply. "Like what?"

Kenny kept his head down. "Nothing special." He stood up. "Okay, I'm ready."

The stethoscope was cold on Kenny's bare chest, and he shivered. "Breathe in," Dr. Hayakawa said. He cocked his head, looking aside. "Out." He moved the stethoscope. "In." All the while, Mom, sitting in a chair beside the examination table, rubbed one thumb over the other, the way she always did when she was nervous.

Kenny continued to breathe in and out on command. He'd been through this dozens of times. He knew this examination room like his own bedroom: the eye chart on the wall, the glass jars of cotton balls and tongue depressors, the standing scale with the measuring rod that Dr. Hayakawa always moved down, down, down to the top of his head, confirming, once again, that he was short for his age.

Kenny had had rheumatic fever as a little boy. He didn't ember much about the actual illness, only lying in bed, ing with fever, aching all over, his throat sore. He remembered Mom and Dad hovering over him, sponging him with cool cloths that gave him goose bumps.

It was only afterward, after he'd gotten better, that the trouble had started. Dr. Hayakawa had listened to his chest for what seemed like forever, telling Kenny to breathe in, breathe out, hold his breath, cough. Kenny remembered the doctor's furrowed forehead as he'd moved the stethoscope and listened, moved it to another spot and listened.

"I think I detect a heart murmur," Dr. Hayakawa had said, and Kenny could still remember the sound of Mom's gasp, the way Dad's face fell. "It is very slight. It may mean nothing." The doctor paused. "It may be serious. I can't say."

"But I feel fine," Kenny had said.

The doctor had shaken his head. "That is the cruelty of this condition. It is silent. It progresses slowly. A weakened valve, a slow leak." He bowed. "I am sorry."

Kenny had had innumerable doctor's visits ever since. Always the same routine. Always the same conclusion: "I think I detect a murmur. I can't be sure. Better be careful, just in case."

To Mom and Dad, *better be careful* meant *do nothing*. No running. No roller-skating. *No baseball.*

"Take it easy." "Don't overdo it." "Sit and rest." That was all he'd heard since then, all he'd been allowed to do. So he'd sat with a book. Sat and kept score while the other kids played. Sat. Sat. Sat. Never dared to test, to push.

Now, Dr. Hayakawa removed the stethoscope from his ears and turned to Mom.

"Everything is the same, Mrs. Sakamoto. Certainly no worse. But still, very faint, I think I hear a slight abnormality in the heartbeat." He placed his hand on Kenny's shoulder. "Keep taking it easy, young man. That's the safest way."

He bowed to Mom. She bowed back. "Thank you, doctor."

On the way home, Mom said, "Nothing worse. That's good news, eh, Kenny?"

"Mmm-hmm," Kenny murmured. But he was thinking about what Dr. Hayakawa had said. "Keep taking it easy."

Not anymore.

2

When they got home, there was a note from Mickey on the kitchen table. *At the gym. Be back soon. Sally is playing with Gittie at Auntie Miriam's.*

Good, Kenny thought. *Gives me a chance to set up my plan.* He waited for Mom to go into the bathroom, then fetched his and Mickey's baseball gloves, a ball and a bat. "Just going out for a little while, Mom. When Mickey gets back, tell him to wait for me, okay?"

"What are you up to, Kenny?" Mom called from behind the closed door.

Pretending not to hear, Kenny slipped out the front door and hurried down the street. He walked several blocks, searching for the right spot.

It has to be out of the way. A place where no nosy neighbors will chance by. Maybe by the railroad tracks . . .

Kenny turned down Main Street. He slipped his

hand inside his glove. *His* glove—that was a joke. It was an old hand-me-down of Mickey's, and Kenny had hardly ever used it. The leather was soft and worn, a rich golden-tan; Kenny kept it supple with neatsfoot oil, even though he had never played a game with it. He stretched his fingers. The inside felt smooth, comfortable. Like it belonged on his hand.

Half an hour later, he was back. Mickey, flushed and sweaty, was standing in the front hall. "But I had a team workout, Mom," he was saying.

Mom frowned. "I thought the Asahis' season was over."

"Yeah, but we're getting in shape for next year."

Kenny fidgeted.

Mom put her hands on her hips. "You'd better not neglect your schoolwork, Mickey."

"School hasn't even started yet, Mom!"

"Yes, and I know what happens. Baseball this and baseball that, and no time for studies."

"I'll keep up. I promise."

"You'd better, young man."

As soon as Mom went into the kitchen, Kenny led his brother down the front steps. Looking both ways down

Alexander Street to make sure no one could hear, he said, "Mickey, you've got to help me."

Mickey looked alarmed. "It's not your heart, is it?"

Kenny almost laughed. *Yes—but not in the way you think.* "No, I'm fine."

"Whew," Mickey said. "So, what is it?"

Before Kenny could answer, he heard, "Yoo-hoo! Boys!"

He looked up. Auntie Miriam was waving from her front step next door. Her thin, slightly hooked nose was sunburned from the game the day before, and her wavy dark hair was pulled into a loose bun. Sally, Kenny's six-year-old sister, and Gittie, Auntie Miriam's five-and-a-half-year-old daughter, were sitting on the top step, playing with paper dolls.

Auntie Miriam and Uncle Jake Bernstein weren't really the Sakamotos' aunt and uncle. They were Mom and Dad's best friends. Sally and Brigitte, or Gittie, as she was usually called, were best friends, too. Susana, the Bernsteins' older daughter, was Kenny's best friend. Kenny and Susana told each other everything. But right now Kenny hoped Susana wasn't around. What he was about to ask Mickey had to be a secret.

Thankfully Susana wasn't in sight.

Auntie Miriam came down the stairs. "Mazel tov, Mickey," she said.

"Thanks, Auntie Miriam."

"Such a hit. Like a cannon. I thought my heart was going to pop right out of my chest. And Jake was squeezing my hand so hard I'm blue and black."

The boys laughed.

Auntie Miriam looked closely at Kenny. "You feeling good, Kenny?"

"Fine, thanks."

"Good, good." She nodded. "You boys got any room for some rugelach, just out of the oven?"

"Sure!"

"Wait. In one second I'm back." She came out with a plate of tiny rolled pastries. Steam arose from their crisp crusts. Kenny inhaled the cinnamon.

"Mmm, thanks, Auntie Miriam." Walnuts, raisins and sugar melted in his mouth.

"Where are you two going?" Sally called.

"Nowhere," Kenny answered, and, before Sally could ask anything else, he guided Mickey down the street.

"Okay, Kenny, what is it?" Mickey said, licking his fingers.

"I need you to help—"

"There's Mickey!"

Kenny looked up. Several of his classmates were running over. They pumped Mickey's hand and asked for his autograph. Blushing, Mickey signed slips of paper. Then more neighbors approached.

"It's the nimble Nippon!" someone said, and everyone laughed. That was what a newspaper reporter had called Mickey when he stole two bases in one game, and the nickname had stuck.

"Great game, Mickey!"

"Such glory for the Asahis!"

"How'd you come up with that massive line drive, Mickey?"

Mickey ducked his head. "It was a lucky hit. I was as surprised as anyone. But my hit was just one small part. It was a team victory. I am proud to have contributed."

Kenny shook his head. Of course Mickey said that. No Asahi player would brag about himself. But Kenny knew better. He'd known all season that his big brother had that kind of hit in him. It was only a matter of time before it burst out.

Mickey bowed to the crowd, and finally Kenny was able to move him on.

"Sorry, Kenny." Mickey linked arms with his brother. "What do you need help with?"

Kenny opened his mouth to answer, but was distracted by a rasping sound. He and Mickey were passing a shop called Saxony Meats, and the owner, a white man, was sweeping the sidewalk out front. He glared at them, then swept a pile of refuse right at them. Dust swirled around their ankles.

"Move along, Japs," he said, waving the broom.

Kenny stood there, his mouth open. This rarely happened, but when it did, it always took him by surprise. Now that he thought of it, it had been happening more often lately.

Mickey took his arm and pulled him away. "Don't pay attention."

Kenny let himself be led.

"Now," Mickey said, "what were you going to tell me?"

Kenny waited until they had crossed Gore Street. "I want you to help me try out for the Clovers."

"What? You can't do that! And Mom and Dad would kill me if I let you try."

"They don't have to know."

"Kenny! Besides, you aren't supposed to run around. What if . . . ?" Mickey's voice trailed off.

"My heart is fine!" Kenny snapped.

That wasn't what Dr. Hayakawa had said. But right now Kenny didn't care. He was sick of sitting out. Sick of not being allowed to play the game he loved. Sick of watching the other kids ride bikes, climb trees, roller-skate, race in the alleys. Sick of being the biggest Asahi fan in Vancouver but never having a hope of *being* an Asahi.

"But, Kenny," Mickey said, "the doctor said no exertion."

"He didn't say I have to sit like a bump on a log for the rest of my life! He just said I have to be careful. And I will. I'll stop the first minute I feel anything. I promise."

Mickey shook his head. "I can't let you take the chance. I know it's no fun for you, but—"

"No, you don't!"

Mickey stopped, looking surprised.

"You don't know," Kenny repeated angrily. "It's so easy for you. You're so good. Always were. How'd you like to dream of something you can't have? To be on the Clovers. Not even be a star, just wear the uniform." He swallowed. "I know I'll never make it anyway, Mickey—"

"Don't say that."

Kenny knew the truth. He didn't have a chance. After years of doing practically nothing, he was weak. He could barely lift a bat, let alone swing it. Riding his bike, he had to get off and walk it up even small hills. Even Susana could beat him.

Learn to hit a line drive, steal a base, outrun a cut-off throw, leap up to catch a high fly ball? And do it all in the six months before the Clovers' tryouts? Hopeless.

But still . . .

"I've got to try. Don't you see, Mickey?"

"But even if I said I'd help you train—and I'm not saying I am, so don't get any ideas—there's no way we could do it without Mom and Dad knowing. The Powell Street Grounds is right in the middle of everything. They'd never let you—"

"Ah, but we're not going to do it at the Powell Street Grounds." With a sly smile, Kenny led his brother north on Main Street, and then across the railroad tracks. On the other side of Waterfront Road, Main Street curved away to the west, and in the half-circle created by the curve and Waterfront Road, there was a dusty stretch of grass about the size of Kenny's school playground. Dotted with weeds, bare patches and the occasional fist-sized rock, it was empty, flat—and hidden from the rest of the neighborhood by a line of railroad sheds. "We're going to do it here." Pushing aside a scraggly bush, he pulled out the bat, ball and gloves he'd hidden earlier.

Mickey wagged his finger. "You sneak! You've thought of everything, haven't you?"

Kenny grinned. "Yup. This place is perfect, isn't it?"

"Yeah, but—"

"Please, Mickey. I can't do it without you."

Mickey crushed a clod of earth in his hand, watching the dirt sift through his fingers. He looked at his brother for a long moment. "You're going to have to work—hard."

Kenny squelched a smile. "I will."

"Run laps."

"I know."

"Field grounders and fly balls until you're blue in the face."

The smile escaped. "Okay." Kenny threw his arms around his brother. "Thanks, Mickey!"

Despite a voice telling him to forget it, that he'd never make the Clovers, he could already see himself in uniform, wearing a crisp cap with a *C* on it, holding a bat over his shoulder, his mitt dangling from the end.

And his father, watching from the sidelines, the same look on his face as when he watched Mickey, saying to the person next to him, "That's my son. Kenji. My boy."

"All right then," Mickey said. "You want to start with hitting or fielding?"

"Hitting," Kenny answered, imagining himself clouting a line drive like the one Mickey had hit the day before.

"Okay." Mickey lifted the bat and held it easily over his shoulder. "There are two main rules. One: keep your eye on the ball. Two: keep the bat level. Watch." In one fluid motion, he brought his arms around, the back wrist following the front wrist on a level line, his hips pivoting while his back foot stayed in place. "See? You don't have to clobber it. Just smooth and level. Meet the ball."

Mickey swung again. It looked easy. Smooth and level, just like he said.

"Right."

"Okay. Take a few practice swings. No ball. Just swing."

Kenny held the bat over his shoulder. It wobbled. He tried to hold it steady.

"Choke up a bit," Mickey said, showing Kenny how to move his hands up toward the fat part of the bat.

That was better. Kenny took a breath, then swung. The bat dipped to waist height before coming back up.

"Keep it level," Mickey said. "Imagine you're coming around on a tabletop, nice and flat."

Kenny raised the bat again. This time he concentrated on keeping the swing flat. The bat dipped, though not as far.

"That's better," Mickey said. "Again."

Kenny swung again, and again. He managed not to let the bat drop too much, but his arms started trembling. He lowered the bat and leaned on it, trying to look casual, like he'd seen other boys do when chatting between innings.

"Okay," Mickey said, "now let's try it with the ball."

He lobbed the ball slowly. Kenny watched it as it left Mickey's hand, but, switching his attention to the bat, he lost concentration and swung a foot beneath the ball.

"That's all right," Mickey said as Kenny ran to retrieve the ball. "Try again."

This time Kenny's swing went over the ball and sliced downward. He felt his cheeks burn.

"Watch the ball all the way in," Mickey said. "Keep the bat level. Tabletop."

Kenny missed again, underneath. He ran a little slower for the ball.

"You're coming closer," Mickey said kindly.

Kenny's eyes stung. *I'm not. Mickey's just being nice.*

Again he missed. He huffed, trotting after the ball, then switched to a walk.

Again.

Chasing the ball to throw it back, Kenny felt his breath coming hard. His heartbeat pounded in his ears. He tried to turn away from Mickey, but his brother said sharply, "Kenny! You're all red in the face."

"I'm okay—"

"No, you're not. Cripes, Kenny, you should have told me you were tired."

"But . . ." *But I need the practice*, Kenny thought. *Desperately.*

"That's it for today. Come on."

They gathered up the equipment and started walking home. Kenny's shoulders slumped. This was a rotten idea. What had ever made him think he could make the Clovers? They were the elite of the nine- to eleven-year-olds. Boys from all over Vancouver tried out. Boys who had played baseball from the time they were out of diapers. Meanwhile, he couldn't even swing a bat. His legs were tired, and his arms felt like *udon* noodles.

The image of himself in a Clovers uniform, of the bat perched on his shoulder, of Dad looking on proudly, vanished.

3

A week later, Kenny and Susana sat on the bottom step of Susana's front stairs. Kenny opened his lunch box. "What have you got today?"

Susana unlatched her lunch box and handed him something wrapped in waxed paper. "Oatmeal cookie."

"Yum!" Kenny tucked it into his lunch box and handed her a round package.

"*Mochi*!" Susana cried. "I love your mama's *mochi*." She unwrapped the corner and took a tiny bite. "Mmm . . ." With a sigh, she put the rest away.

They started walking to school. "Did you get the arithmetic problems?" Susana asked.

"No, did you?"

"I hate word problems," Susana said. "If John can pick fourteen bushels of apples an hour—"

"Then he's Superman. He can rip up the tree and shake all the apples down."

Susana laughed and her dark eyes sparkled. "And we don't have to do any multiplication."

Her family had come to Canada when Susana was four and Auntie Miriam was expecting Gittie. They had moved into the house next door to the Sakamotos. As they later laughingly told Kenny's family, a distant cousin had found them a place to live in Vancouver; they'd had no idea it was in the middle of the Japanese community and had been amazed to see so many Asian people in the neighborhood. And Mom told them, "We were surprised to see a white family move in!"

Mom, hugely pregnant with Sally at the time, had gone over with a pot of *udon* soup and a plate of green tea cakes. That was the beginning of the friendship between the two families. Kenny and Susana, and, later, Sally and Gittie, had grown up together, lost teeth together, had chicken pox together. Kenny hadn't thought anything of having a girl for a best friend—and a white Jewish girl at that—until he started school. But when the other kids said to him, "What are you playing with her for? You want to be with the girls?" and after

Susana heard the same thing on her side, they'd quickly realized that it wasn't the thing to be seen as best friends.

Now, a block away from the massive brick walls of Lord Strathcona School, they stopped. Susana skipped ahead and caught up with a group of girls walking together. Kenny waited a moment, watching her curly, dark brown pigtails bounce with each skip, then met a group of boys on the corner.

Miss Morfitt clapped her hands. "All right, boys and girls, line up in two rows. Since it's such a nice day, we'll take our physical education class outside."

"Yay!" several children called.

Kenny lined up silently. It was the second week of grade four, and he had already given Miss Morfitt the note from Mom, the same note he gave his teacher every year.

Dear Miss Morfitt,

Please excuse my son Kenji Sakamoto from physical education. He has a heart defect and is not allowed to take vigorous exercise.

Yours truly,
Mrs. Keiko Sakamoto

The children filed outside, and after Miss Morfitt had formed them into two teams for kickball, she approached Kenny. "Kenny, would you like to keep score?"

No, I would not, Kenny thought. "Sure," he said.

Miss Morfitt smiled, handing him paper and pencil. Kenny sat on the grass along the third baseline. He wrote "Team 1" and "Team 2" at the top of two columns, then drew horizontal lines and numbered five innings.

Tak Watanabe swaggered up to the plate, wearing his Clovers baseball cap. "Hat, Tak," Miss Morfitt scolded, and Tak, with a smirk, stuffed his cap into his back pocket. *Show-off*, Kenny thought.

Naomi Tanaka, pitching for the other team, rolled Tak the ball. He gave it a mighty kick. The ball sailed into right field, where Kenny's friend, tall, lanky Dai Kimura, was positioned.

"Go, Tak!" his teammates called.

As Tak rounded first base and headed for second, Dai held up both arms. He missed. The ball flew over his head and rolled away on the gravelly sand of the playing field. Dai pushed up his glasses and loped after it. His teammates groaned. Tak sped toward third base. Dai scooped up the ball and feebly threw it infield. Susana, who was playing second base, picked it up and heaved it toward home. Too late. Tak tagged as the catcher jumped up to catch the ball.

"Home run!" Tak punched an arm in the air and his teammates cheered.

Dai trudged back out to right field. *Poor guy,* Kenny thought.

Grudgingly, Kenny marked a run in the Team 1 column. Of course Tak had scored. He was the best athlete in the class. When the tryouts for the Clovers had been held last spring, in March, there were only a handful of boys in Kenny's class who had already turned nine and were old enough to try out. Only one of them—Tak—had made it. Midway through the Clovers' season, leading the team in hits—as a nine-year-old!—he had bragged to his friends, with Kenny standing right there, "People say I'm the next Mickey Sakamoto."

But I'm *Mickey's brother*, Kenny had thought. I *should be the next Mickey Sakamoto.* There was only one problem. It was true. Tak was that talented.

Now, watching Tak trot off the field, Kenny thought with dismay, *I'm going to have to compete against him to win a spot on the Clovers.*

The next player also kicked the ball toward Dai, who misplayed that one, too. Susana made the next two outs, but the next player singled, and the one after that doubled. By the time the half-inning was over, Team 1 had five points.

With burly Keith McAlary pitching, Susana made a triple. Keith glared at her, then snapped at the left fielder, "You should have had that."

Go, Susana, Kenny thought.

The next player connected, and Susana ran home to score. In the Team 2 column, Kenny marked the run, shading it with his pencil until it was dark and thick.

Dai came up. All the fielders moved in. Dai's first kick missed the ball. "Put on your glasses, Kimura," Tak hooted from second base. "Oh, wait, you already have them on."

"That's enough, Tak," Miss Morfitt said sharply.

Kenny felt sorry for Dai. Brilliant at schoolwork, yes, but he *was* clumsy, and he took a lot of teasing.

Dai connected on the next kick, but the ball only rolled feebly toward the pitcher. Keith easily threw it to his buddy Eddie Pavlich at first base for the out.

Shrugging, Dai came and sat next to Kenny. The two boys, left out of games, often sat together. "I'm not very good," Dai said quietly.

"Kickball isn't everything. You're good at other things. Like math."

Dai brightened. "Math is easy."

"For you, maybe," Kenny said. "I bet you know exactly how many apples John picked."

"Eighty-four bushels."

Kenny laughed. "See?"

The third out was made, and the teams switched sides. Dai returned to the outfield.

By the time the game was over, Team 1 had won, 12–5. But two of Team 2's runs, scored by Susana, stood out dark and bold on the page.

The children lined up to go back inside. Chatting with Dai, Kenny took his place in the boys' line. Susana, her skirt dusty and one curly pigtail drooping, stood across from him in the girls' line. Kenny heard Keith and Eddie talking behind him.

"The Jerries are bombing the heck out of London . . . ," Eddie was saying.

"Yeah, three RAF planes were shot down," Keith said.

Kenny ignored them. The two boys were obsessed with

the war. Of course, everyone was—with Canadian troops on the front lines in Europe, it was impossible not to be. But Keith and Eddie seemed to delight in the carnage, constantly citing the number of bombs dropped, troops slaughtered, civilians killed.

"My dad said it was the biggest German attack yet," Eddie added.

Susana turned at the word *German*.

"What are you looking at, you dirty Kraut?" Keith said.

Susana's mouth fell open.

Without thinking, Kenny turned. "Don't you call her that."

"You going to stop me?" Keith taunted.

"Yeah!" Kenny gave Keith a shove. Keith staggered back, crashing into Eddie.

"Why, you . . ."

"Kenny, don't!" Susana screamed.

Keith, a head taller than Kenny and with hands the size of soup bowls, grabbed him by the shirt. Rearing back with one arm, Keith punched him in the face.

Kenny heard the crack of knuckles on cheekbone. "Ow!" he said. He raised his arm, but before he could swing, Eddie, short but muscular, head-butted him. Kenny fell, knocking Dai over with him. Dai's glasses went flying. Several girls started screaming.

"Stop this at once!" Miss Morfitt yelled.

Fist at the ready, Keith froze. He lowered his arm. Eddie stepped back in line, tucking in his shirt. Someone gave Kenny a hand up, and Kenny, in turn, helped Dai. Susana handed Dai his glasses.

Kenny put a hand to his cheek. It was wet. Blood.

"What is going on?" Miss Morfitt said.

There was silence.

"Kenny, I'm surprised," Miss Morfitt said. "This isn't like you. What happened?"

"Nothing, Miss Morfitt." He wasn't going to tattle.

"Keith?"

"Nothing."

Another silence.

Naomi put up her hand. "Keith called Susana"—she started to explain, then lowered her voice and finished—"a dirty Kraut."

Susana, staring straight ahead, turned bright red.

Miss Morfitt frowned. "Into the classroom, all of you. Kenny, go clean up and then join us."

Kenny examined himself in the bathroom mirror. The bleeding had stopped; now he had a raw-looking scrape across his cheekbone. *My first fight*, he thought with pride. Then, *Mom's going to kill me*.

Miss Morfitt was sitting on the edge of her desk. The class was silent.

"Keith, can you tell us what a Kraut is?"

"A German. And they're our enemy—"

"That will do. Susana, are you a Kraut?"

Susana blushed. "Well, we did come from Germany." She turned and looked at Keith. "But we're not *for* the Germans! We're against them."

Miss Morfitt spoke softly. "Would you mind telling the class why your family left Germany, Susana? This may be private. Only if you want to."

Susana took a breath. Kenny knew this was hard for her. The Bernsteins didn't talk about it much. He knew why they'd left Germany, but not many of the other children did.

"Because we're Jews," she said. "Because the Nazis shut down our schools. They burned down our synagogue. They put a rock through the window of my papa's store." Her voice trembled. "We were lucky to escape."

The room was silent.

"Thank you, Susana," Miss Morfitt said. "Keith, do you have anything to say?"

"Sorry," Keith said in a sullen voice. Kenny knew he didn't mean it.

"I hope so," Miss Morfitt said. "I will see you after school. You, too, Kenny. Even if you were defending your friend, we cannot have fighting in the playground."

Mom's really *going to kill me*, Kenny thought.

Susana was waiting for him when Miss Morfitt finally dismissed him. He and Keith had both been assigned lines to write on the blackboard: "I will not fight in the school yard." Keith was still in there writing his.

"I never knew you could fight," Susana said.

Kenny gave a shaky laugh. "I can't. I didn't even land a punch."

"You stood up to that creep. That counts."

They turned down their street and paused in front of their houses. "Will you be okay?" Susana asked.

"Yeah."

"Thanks, Kenny," Susana said.

"That's all right—"

"I mean it."

Kenny tried to sneak down the hall to his room, but Mom came out of the kitchen. She wore a flowered apron she had made, and her black hair, normally neat in a short bob, was slightly curled from the steam of whatever she was cooking. "Kenny, where were you? You're late—" She sucked in her breath. "What happened to you?"

"It's nothing, Mom."

"Did you fall?"

"No. Uh . . . some kids were picking on Susana."

Mom's eyes widened. "You were . . . *in a fight*?"

"Yes, Mom."

Mom grabbed him by the shoulders. Kenny expected her to yell, but instead her face took on the concerned look he knew so well. "Kenny, you mustn't get overexcited. You know it's not good for your heart."

"I'm fine, Mom, really—"

"Promise me, Kenny. Promise you won't do it again. You can't take the chance."

Kenny sighed. "Promise."

She held him close.

When she finally released him, Kenny went into the bathroom. The scrape was beginning to scab over, and the area just above his cheekbone was turning a faint purple.

It created a lump on his already-chubby face, as if he'd tucked a plum inside his cheek. *Soft*, Mom called him. *Flabby*, he called himself. *A shrimp*. Short and round, like Mom, not tall and lean like Mickey and Dad.

It's almost funny, he thought. *I got in trouble not for fighting, but for overdoing it. Typical.*

Still, he was proud of his bruised cheek. "My first combat wound," he said to his reflection.

4

"A toast," Uncle Jake said, raising his sake cup. "To the Rookie of the Year." It was early October, and the evening sun slanted into the room, making his reddish beard shine golden, as if reflecting the colors of the falling leaves outside.

Kenny's and Susana's families were gathered around the Sakamotos' dining room table. They took turns every Friday night: one week at Susana's, when Auntie Miriam lit the Shabbos candles and served her delicious roasted chicken, with honey cake for dessert, and one week at Kenny's, when Mom made her Japanese specialties.

A few days earlier, the Vancouver newspapers had named Mickey the outstanding rookie of the 1941 Asahi team and had predicted great things for the "nimble Nippon." On the street, Mickey hadn't been able to go anywhere without well-wishers slapping him on the back and shaking his hand.

Dad, Mom and Auntie Miriam clinked cups. Across the table, Sally and Gittie did the same with their water glasses and giggled as if they were drinking sake. Mickey looked down modestly, but Kenny could see the gleam under his eyelids. "Thanks, Uncle Jake. It's an incredible honor. I don't deserve it, but—"

"Baloney!" Susana said.

"Susana!" Auntie Miriam scolded. "Language."

"Sorry, Mama. But it's true, Mickey. You were far and away the best rookie, and don't try to deny it."

Mickey's mouth twitched. Kenny could tell he was struggling not to grin.

As Mom and Auntie Miriam went into the kitchen to bring in the dinner, Uncle Jake turned to Dad. "All the papers are saying that Mickey may be the first Japanese to break into the major leagues. Wouldn't that be something, Harry?"

Dad beamed. "You bet."

"Who would you like to play for, Mickey? The Yankees? The Dodgers? The Cardinals?"

"Go for the Dodgers, Mickey," Susana said. "They were good this year."

Kenny nodded. "First pennant in twenty-one years."

"They still lost to the Yankees in the World Series," Dad said.

"They always lose to the Yankees," Susana said. "They need you, Mickey."

"I'd go anywhere to play in the majors," Mickey said with a grin. "But I still have a few more years on the Asahis first."

"What's all this?" Mom said, coming back into the dining room with a platter of yakitori chicken. "Mickey is going straight to university when he graduates. We've talked about this, Harry."

Dad looked sheepish. "Now, Keiko, education is important, of course it is. But if Mickey has a chance to play professional ball first, and they allowed Japanese—"

"University," Mom repeated, pointing at Mickey. "Not gallivanting off to some strange American city to play baseball."

Mickey put up his hands. "I'm not gallivanting anywhere, Mom. Just back to the Asahis in the spring."

"Yes. In the spring. So why are you always at the gym now, I'd like to know, when you should be studying—"

"But imagine if he got signed by the Yankees," Dad whispered to Uncle Jake. "Playing alongside Joe DiMaggio—"

"Harry!" Mom snapped.

Everyone laughed.

Mom and Auntie Miriam went back and forth, bringing in platters. The table was set with Mom's special tablecloth, the one on which she had embroidered yellow cranes, and her good china, the gold-rimmed plates with a pinecone design, which she had brought from Japan when she came to marry Dad. Kenny loved those pinecones, the spray of green and brown on the plate, but they soon disappeared under helpings of food. In addition to the chicken, there was rice, yam tempura, cucumber and daikon salad, and carrot and cabbage *tsukemono.* Kenny loved alternating bites of the sweet yams and the tangy *tsukemono* pickles.

Uncle Jake raised his sake cup again. "Another toast. To Kenny."

Kenny looked up in confusion. "Me? What for?"

"Coming to Susana's defense."

"What's this?" Dad said.

Mom's face turned red. "I didn't want to worry you, Harry—"

"It was nothing, Dad," Kenny said quickly.

"*Kenny?*"

While Kenny blushed, Susana told Dad about the incident in the playground.

"Thank you, Kenny," Auntie Miriam said. "Brave, it was."

"Brave!" Dad said. He turned to Kenny. "You know you're not supposed to roughhouse."

"I know, Dad—"

"I don't think you need to worry, Harry," Uncle Jake said.

"But the doctor said—"

"Sure, sure," Uncle Jake interrupted. "But look at him. He looks fine." His tone softened. "Let him be a boy."

Auntie Miriam said something to Uncle Jake. It wasn't in German, but in that other language they spoke, Yiddish. Uncle Jake turned to Mom and Dad with an apologetic look. "I hereby stop butting in where my opinion is not wanted."

Everyone laughed. Uncle Jake winked at Kenny. Kenny grinned back. Sometimes he thought Uncle Jake and Auntie Miriam understood him better than Mom and Dad did. They didn't see him as a weak little boy; he was just Kenny.

The conversation turned to politics, as it often did when grown-ups got together, and Kenny tuned out, gazing at the mantel. It was lined with a runner that Mom had made by sewing colorful scraps of material together in a zigzag pattern, and on it sat two photographs.

One was a picture Dad had taken of the memorial to Japanese Canadian soldiers in Stanley Park. Dad had many more of his photos hanging in his store, Sakamoto Photo, but this was Kenny's favorite. Not just because the memorial was important to Dad, since he had fought for Canada in the Great War, but because the picture was beautiful. Dad had taken it at night. The memorial's spire rose straight and tall, like a soldier standing at attention, and the eternal flame inside the lantern at the top sent shards of light into the black sky.

Kenny remembered asking Dad why he had opened a camera store instead of becoming a fisherman in Steveston, like his father. Dad had told him that that was just what he had planned to do. But while he was away fighting for Canada, his father had died in a tragic fishing accident, and his mother had forbidden him to go to sea. "I'd always loved taking pictures and tinkering with cameras, so I opened the store," he had told Kenny. That was nearly twenty years ago, and now Sakamoto Photo was one of the best-known stores on Powell Street. Mickey worked there after school, partly to help Dad out and partly to save for baseball expenses.

Kenny's eyes roved to the other photograph. It was a picture of the family. Kenny remembered when they'd had it taken, a year earlier. Mom and Dad had sat in chairs, like in traditional Japanese portraits Kenny had seen, with the elders seated, Dad in a suit and tie, his face solemn and proud, Mom in a formal dress with a string of pearls, her hair artificially curled around her chubby face. The three children—Mickey in a suit, only fifteen but already as tall as a man, Sally in a frilly dress with a big bow in her poker-straight black hair, and Kenny in a button-down shirt and pressed slacks, the tuft of hair that always stuck up in the back slicked down with water—stood behind them, half-smiling as if not sure whether to be serious or joyous. *My family*, he thought.

For dessert, Mom served her *manjū* cakes along with green tea. The sweetness of red bean paste flooded Kenny's mouth. "Mmm, Mom, you make the best *manjū*."

Susana simply held out her plate. "More, please, Auntie Keiko?"

Mom beamed. Meanwhile, Sally and Gittie were whispering and giggling.

"What are you two up to?" Susana said.

"It's a surprise," Sally said, taking Gittie's hand. "Wait here. We'll be right back."

A few minutes later, there was a clomp-clomp down the hall, and Sally and Gittie appeared, dressed in Sally's kimonos, with obi sashes tied crookedly around their waists and wooden geta on their feet. Both of their mouths were smears of bright red.

"Sakura Sakamoto, what are you doing with lipstick on?" Mom scolded. But when Auntie Miriam stifled a giggle, Mom laughed, too. "That is coming right off when this is over, young lady."

"Yes, Mommy." Sally stepped forward. "Presenting . . . Sakura Sakamoto and Brigitte Bernstein, performing a special *odori* dance!"

"This should be good, since Gittie has no idea what *odori* is," Susana whispered to Kenny.

The two girls struck up positions with their hands clasped together and their eyes cast down. Mickey put the record player on. When the flute started playing its high, lonely sound, Sally swept her arm across her body. Gittie, watching Sally out of the corner of her eye, copied the motion a second later. Sally twirled. Gittie tried to twirl, but she bumped into Sally, who stumbled and stepped out of her geta. Giggling, she wiggled her foot back in. She shuffled with tiny steps to the left. When Gittie followed, Sally said in a loud stage whisper, "The other way!"

Kenny snorted into his hand. He glanced at Susana. Her nostrils were twitching.

Gittie, looking over her shoulder to see what to do next, fell over. Sally fell on top of her. The two girls lay in a heap, laughing. They jumped up and, raising clasped hands, made a deep bow.

"Bravo!" Dad said as everyone applauded.

"Very good, girls," Mom said. "Now, go wash off that lipstick."

Sally and Gittie clomped down the hall.

Mom rolled her eyes. "What a pair of show-offs."

"True," Auntie Miriam said. "But you know, Keiko, I think Sally has talent. She's graceful."

"If you call falling on the floor graceful," Kenny said.

"What she really likes best about *odori* is the costume," Mom said. "You should see her parading in front of the mirror before class."

Auntie Miriam laughed. "Sure, it's all about the glamor now. But she may surprise you."

Sally and Gittie skipped back into the room, their mouths shadowed with faint red.

"That's better," Mom said.

"Let's go for a walk," Dad said. "We can go down by the water. There's just enough light to take a group picture and get back before dark."

Five minutes later, they were strolling along. They swung up to Powell Street, to Sakamoto Photo, so Dad could pick up a special camera he wanted to use. Then, since it was a mild fall evening, they first walked to Woodward's department store on Hastings Street.

The window was filled with posters. SUPPORT THE WAR EFFORT—BUY VICTORY BONDS! shouted one. Another showed men and women soldiers marching shoulder to shoulder, urging women to join the Canadian Women's Army Corps. Behind the posters, mannequins wearing gas masks demonstrated what to do in case of an air raid. A sign warned passersby to BE PREPARED!

"It's not going well over there," Auntie Miriam said in a low voice. "Hitler's army keeps advancing into Russia. They've marched almost to Moscow."

Kenny knew that she was worried about her family. The Bernsteins still had relatives in Germany. None had been heard from in over a year.

"So you'd think we'd take Nikkei volunteers, wouldn't you?" Dad said.

"What do you mean, Dad?" Kenny asked.

Dad turned to him. "The Canadian Forces won't allow Japanese to enlist."

"Why not?"

"They say they can't be sure of our loyalty."

"That's crazy," Mickey said. "Look at all the Japanese who fought for Canada in the last war."

"That's what makes it so maddening," Dad agreed. "Of course we're loyal. We're Canadian!"

"Why no Japanese?" Kenny asked. "We're at war with Germany, not Japan."

"Yes, but the way Japan's been rolling over Asia, the government's obviously afraid that they'll launch an attack against the West," Dad said.

"Don't say that!" Mom said. "I'm so worried about *Okaasan* and *Otousan*. Oh, I wish they had come here when they had the chance."

Kenny felt a pang. He knew that Mom's parents had stayed behind in Japan when Mom had moved to Canada to marry Dad. He barely knew those grandparents, having met them only once on a visit to Japan when he was three. Vaguely he remembered a short couple in a tiny house cluttered with figurines of ancient warriors and long scrolls depicting clouds and mountains, and the scratchy fabric of his grandmother's dress as she hugged him, the smell of ink on his grandfather's fingers.

"Don't worry, Keiko," Dad said. "It won't come to that."

"I'd enlist," Mickey said.

"You'll do no such thing," Mom said. "Anyway, you're underage."

"That didn't stop Dad." Mickey smiled.

"I never should have told you that." Dad chuckled, then grew serious. "It's no laughing matter. War is not a joke."

"I know," Mickey said. "We had an air raid drill at school, with gas masks and everything."

Sally pointed at the mannequins. "Like that?"

Mickey nodded.

Sally stamped her foot. "I am *not* wearing one of those.

They're too ugly."

Everyone laughed. They turned north, toward the waterfront. Dad unscrewed the lens cap on his camera. "Squish together, everybody."

Before they got into position, two Royal Canadian Mounted Police officers stepped in front of them. The older one put out his hand. "Identity cards, please."

Dad frowned. "Is that necessary, officer? We're just out for an evening stroll."

"I don't care what you're doing, sir. You Japs need to show me your identity cards."

The other policeman, Kenny saw, who was younger, looked uncomfortable at his senior officer's tone.

Dad made to open his mouth, but Mom put her hand on his arm. "Harry."

Clenching his teeth so hard that a muscle in his jaw popped, Dad pulled his card from his wallet. Mom and Mickey withdrew theirs. Kenny and Sally were too young to require them.

Kenny felt Susana stiffen beside him. She had told him about being stopped on the street back in Germany. *Was it like this?*

Tapping the older RCMP officer on the arm, Uncle Jake said, "I want you to know that my friend here is a decorated war vet—"

"That's neither here nor there," the Mountie said. "The government requires all Japanese adults to register, and we are here to enforce the law." He nodded at his partner. "Constable Tait, check their cards."

Kenny's family stood grim and silent as the young officer went down the line. "Thank you, sir. Thank you, ma'am," he said, and tried to smile. When he came to Mickey, he examined the card and then looked up. "Say, you aren't the Mitsuo Sakamoto on the Asahi baseball team, are you? The one who had the winning hit?"

"Yes, I am."

"Holy smokes!" The Mountie held out his hand. "Wait till I tell my pals—"

"Tait!" the older officer barked. "None of that. Finish your job."

The constable reddened. "Yes, sir. All in order, sir."

The older officer nodded. Turning abruptly, he walked away. Constable Tait hurried to catch up. Kenny heard the older officer say, "Arrogant Japs."

"But, sir . . . ," Tait began. His words were lost as they moved away.

A silence fell over the group. Dad screwed the lens cap back on his camera. "Let's go home."

5

When Nakata-sensei, Kenny's Japanese language schoolteacher, wasn't looking, Kenny glanced out the large rectangular window that overlooked Alexander Street. The clouds were low and dark, but it wasn't raining. Yet. *C'mon, bell*, he thought.

Five more excruciating minutes passed by. Finally the bell rang, and Kenny, along with the rest of his class, jumped up. Benches scraped back loudly on the wooden floor.

"*Sayonara*, children. Remember to practice your phrases," Nakata-sensei said, but he said it without hope. In addition to teaching at the Japanese language school, he was also the minister of the United Church that Kenny's family attended. Kenny felt sorry for him. Thin and slight, with stooped shoulders, he had graying hair and a kind expression. He was a good teacher—but no one wanted to be in Japanese school. Not after a whole day of regular school.

Kenny bowed to Nakata-sensei and hurried outside. Mickey would be getting off work in fifteen minutes, and he'd promised they could have another training session if it wasn't raining. Somehow several weeks had slipped by since their last practice, and it was now early November. Yellow cottonwood leaves rustled against the curb, and fresh snow dusted the mountains. Soon it would be too cold and dark to practice at all. The tryouts were in March—only five months away.

Kenny buttoned up his jacket and waited for Sally. *C'mon, c'mon*, he thought, shuffling on the sidewalk. Finally she came, but before Kenny could tear her away, she started a clapping game with her friend Helen. "A sailor went to sea, sea, sea," they chanted, slapping each other's hands in a complicated pattern of straight and diagonal thrusts, "to see what he could see, see—whoops!"

Helen's hand flew past Sally's and hit her in the shoulder. The two girls burst out laughing.

"Silly Billy," Sally said. "Start again. One, two, three—"

"Come on, Sally," Kenny said.

"But all that he could see, see, see—whoops!" Helen missed again.

"Last one!" Kenny threatened.

They completed the rhyme, and finally Kenny managed to deposit Sally at home, drop off his schoolbooks, grab the bat, gloves and ball, and sneak out, all without Mom noticing. He hid the equipment around the side of the shop and went inside.

Dad was behind the counter, talking to a customer. In the glass display case in front of him, a row of the latest cameras and lenses nestled in their boxes. Dad glanced over at Kenny. Immediately, a look of concern crossed his face. Then he nodded, as if reassured, and turned back to the customer.

"This is the best lens on the market, just released by Nikon," he said, holding out the lens. "You get incredible clarity, even at thirty feet. In fact, I took that picture with it."

He pointed to a picture on the wall of a great blue heron soaring over the rocky shore at Coal Harbour, wings spread, long neck outstretched. You could see every feather as if it had been painted on, and the bird's small black eye was a pinpoint of light.

"Amazing!" the customer said. "From thirty feet, you say?"

"Yes. Here, take a look." Fastening the lens to a camera,

Dad handed it over the counter as if he were passing over a baby.

While the customer peered through the viewfinder, Kenny's eyes roved over Dad's other photos on the wall. A close-up of his World War I medal, a star dangling from a striped ribbon, gleaming against a swath of velvet. A shot of an Asahi game at the Powell Street Grounds, taken from high up in the scorekeeper's box, showing a panorama of fans, flags and players in motion, the ball a white blur soaring into the outfield. A picture of fishermen unloading their catch in the early morning fog, their nets bulging with silvery scales, the dock glistening with water droplets.

Kenny spotted Mickey in the photo-developing section at the other end of the shop, where customers dropped off films and picked up their photos. A girl leaned over the counter, holding an envelope of prints. Her black ponytail swept over her shoulder, and dimples creased her cheeks as she talked. Kenny had seen her before. What was her name? Tammy, he remembered. She was the older sister of one of his classmates.

"So . . . Mickey," she said, twirling a bracelet round and round her wrist, "did you hear about the Christmas dance?"

"Uh, yeah," Mickey said.

"And . . . are you going?"

She's got a crush on him, Kenny realized with amusement. He looked at Mickey. His brother didn't seem to have a clue.

Mickey shook his head. "I have a team practice that night."

Tammy looked disappointed. "Oh, really?"

"Can't miss baseball."

"Fine," she snapped. She flounced out of the store.

Mickey, you idiot, Kenny thought. Well, Tammy had just found out about Mickey's true love. And she wasn't the only one. Kenny had seen other girls hanging around the Powell Street Grounds. Mickey always walked right by them, chatting with his Asahi pals.

Mickey closed the cash register and put on his jacket. "I'll be going now, Dad."

"Okay," Dad said. "What are you two up to?"

"Oh, just thought we'd take the long way home," Kenny said. That wasn't a lie, at least.

"All right. See you there. Don't overdo it, Kenny."

"I won't."

Finally! Kenny retrieved the equipment and they hustled to the vacant lot.

"Let's practice bunting today," Mickey said when they arrived. He positioned Kenny where the batter's box would be. "Now, you start with the bat in regular batting position."

"So you don't tip off the pitcher," Kenny said.

"Right. Once the ball leaves the pitcher's hand, bring your back foot around and pivot so you're square to the pitcher. At the same time, slide your upper hand up till your hands are about a foot apart. But keep your fingers pinched behind the bat so they don't get hit. Got that?"

"Uh . . . I think so." Kenny lifted the bat over his shoulder. That was a lot to remember.

"One, two, three," Mickey said, and Kenny swiveled. Moving his back foot was easy. But he was clenching the bat so tightly his right hand barely moved up it.

"Looser. Don't strangle it. Try again."

The next time, his hand moved so far that it nearly slipped off the end of the bat.

"Not so loose."

"Sheesh!"

Kenny tried again. Pivot-step-slide. At first his movements were jerky; the step and the hand-slide were separate. After a few times, though, he began to move more
smoothly, making it one motion.

"That's it," Mickey said. "Now let's try with the ball."
He lobbed the ball. Kenny swiveled into bunt position.
The ball sailed over the bat and hit him in the chest.

"Ow!"

"You okay?"

"Yeah."

Mickey threw again. This time Kenny watched the ball
more closely. He connected—right on top of his fingers,
which were curled around the bat.

"You forgot—"

"Yeah, yeah, I know. Keep them pinched back."

Kenny shook out his hand. Mickey threw. Kenny pivoted, keeping his fingers hidden. He connected. The ball
hit the bat and dribbled a few feet away.

"I did it!"

"You did. Now, try to come around quicker and aim
with the middle of the bat. If you connect with the bottom
end, it won't go anywhere."

Kenny swiveled again. He watched the ball and adjusted the bat so the ball hit higher up. The ball rolled farther.

"Better."

Again and again, Kenny turned and lowered the bat. Most times he hit. He began to feel the rhythm of the pivot and crouch, pivot and crouch.

"Good!" Mickey said. "You've got a feel for it, Kenny."

Kenny beamed. Bunting felt more natural to him than hitting did. He didn't have power, but he did have precision. Positioning the bat just right and feeling the ball career off it felt wonderful. As he and Mickey packed up to leave, he envisioned himself on the Clovers, laying bunts everywhere. He'd continue the Asahi tradition of "brain ball," winning games with great bunting and base running. "He's the next Junji Ito, the new King of Bunting," the fans would say, recalling Kenny's favorite player, one of the greatest Asahis of all time. They'd stop him on the street for his autograph.

He and Mickey were halfway home when a voice called, "Kenny! Mickey!"

Kenny's head jerked up.

Sally!

Sally on roller skates, her arms windmilling, her skirt billowing, her eyes big. She skidded to a stop.

"What are you two doing?"

Kenny felt the blood rush to his face. "Nothing."

"Doesn't look like nothing. You're all dirty." She cocked her head, eyeing the bat. One straight pigtail rose. "You've been playing baseball!"

"No, I was just—"

"Kenny! You know you're not supposed to. I'm telling Mom."

"You wouldn't!" Kenny and Mickey cried together.

Sally seemed to consider. A smile lit her face. "I won't . . . if . . ."

"If what?"

"You buy me a piece of bubble gum. No, two. For when the first one goes flat."

"You blackmailer!" Kenny said.

Sally batted innocent eyes. "I'm just being a good sister. Not tattling."

Kenny snorted.

Sally pushed off, giggling. "Come on, let's go to Morita's Sweet Shop."

Trudging behind her with Mickey, Kenny swore under his breath. Having to bribe his baby sister—how unfair. How embarrassing!

6

Kenny was vaguely aware, on this Sunday in early December, that all around him the congregation was singing. But he wasn't listening. Prayer book open on his lap, his eyes gazing somewhere over Nakata-sensei's shoulder, he was imagining himself coming up to bat in the first game of the Clovers' new season.

The pitcher, Tak Watanabe—somehow Tak got transposed to another team—*throws the ball. Kenny swivels, laying a perfect bunt along the third baseline, and outruns the throw by a whisker. The crowd cheers. A fan says, "That Sakamoto kid is something, isn't he? Reminds me of Junji Ito . . ."*

Kenny felt a poke in his side. Mom nodded toward the pulpit, where Nakata-sensei had bowed his head. Quickly, Kenny bowed his.

"Lord God, protect our brave Canadian Forces and their Allied brethren on the battlefields of Europe. Bring them home safe and sound, and restore peace and loving understanding to your world. Amen."

"Amen," the congregation echoed.

Clothing rustled as people stood up from their pews, hymn books slapped closed and children squealed in celebration of their freedom.

Kenny tapped his foot impatiently as his family stood in a slow-moving line, waiting to shake Nakata-sensei's hand. Mom always cooked a delicious Sunday lunch—today she had promised to make *haru maki*, one of Kenny's favorites. His mouth watered at the thought of the crispy fried wrappers stuffed with crab and shrimp.

As the line snaked forward, Sally found Helen and they resumed their clapping game. "A sailor went to sea, sea, sea . . ." Kenny thought he would scream if he heard it one more time.

Some of Mickey's Asahi pals came over, playfully punching each other in the shoulder. "Hey, Kenny, how's it going?" one of them said.

Kenny's chest puffed up. He loved that the players knew his name. Maybe someday *his* teammates would greet Sally in the same way.

Finally the Sakamotos reached the front of the line, exchanged greetings with Nakata-sensei and his wife, and left. As they walked home, Kenny noticed that there were fewer people on the street, and he could hear the sound of radios from behind closed windows.

"Wonder what's going on," Dad said, climbing the front steps. "Maybe news from the front. I sure hope the Germans haven't entered Moscow."

As soon as he took off his coat and loosened his tie, Dad went into the living room and turned on the radio. Mom put on her apron, and Kenny followed her into the kitchen, hoping to be given the first *haru maki*.

"What!" Dad exclaimed.

Kenny and Mom rushed into the living room.

"The *USS Arizona* immediately became engulfed in flames, along with several other vessels in the American fleet," the announcer was saying. "Hundreds are believed to have died in the surprise attack."

"What is it?" Mom began, but Dad put up his hand for silence. His face was pale.

"Japan declared war on the United Kingdom, Canada and the United States," the announcer went on.

"What?" Mom gasped.

Kenny's stomach clenched. It wasn't so much the announcer's words as the look on Dad's face that scared him.

"In addition to the strike on the American fleet, Japan also invaded Thailand and attacked Malaysia, Singapore and Hong Kong," the announcer said. "World leaders have condemned this hostile provocation—"

"Is lunch ready?" Mickey said, coming into the living room. Then, looking from one parent to the other, asked, "What's going on?"

Dad turned to him with an expression of disbelief. "Japan attacked Pearl Harbor. We're at war."

Kenny's thoughts were in a jumble. *Japan? Attack? War?* "What's Pearl Harbor?"

"The American naval base in Hawaii," Dad answered. "In Honolulu."

"Harry, what does it mean?" Mom asked.

In the background, the announcer droned on. "Casualties . . . international outrage . . . retaliation . . ."

Dad shook his head. "It means the emperor has gone insane."

"But what about *Okaasan* and *Otousan*?" Mom wailed.

All of a sudden Kenny feared for those distant

grandparents. He knew that, over the years, Mom had tried to persuade them to move to Canada. Now her country—his country—was fighting theirs.

Dad patted her shoulder. "I'm sure they're fine, Keiko. Japan may be at war, but it's not on home soil."

"But what if it goes there?" Mom said, rubbing one thumb over the other. "What if we bomb Japan?"

"We'll defeat them before it gets that far, you'll see."

"Do you really think so, Dad?" Mickey asked.

Dad nodded. "Yes, now that the Yanks are in it. We'll go over there and teach Japan a lesson. It'll all be over soon."

"How can we be in two wars at once?" Kenny asked. It seemed so strange. Just yesterday, Canada was in only one war, in Europe. Today there was another, half a world away.

"We fight where our enemies take us." Dad gave a bitter laugh. "They'll be sorry they didn't take Japanese soldiers."

A horrible thought struck Kenny. "Will you have to go and fight?" Because Dad had received a medal for bravery in the Great War, wouldn't the army want him again? He tried to imagine life with Dad. *What will we do? How will we live? And what if . . . he dies?*

"No, I'm too old this time," Dad said. "I'd go if they wanted me—"

"Harry!"

"—but they don't."

The phone rang. Dad answered it. "Yes, Sensei, we heard. . . . Do you really think that's necessary? . . . All right, we'll come."

"Come where?" Mom asked when he hung up.

"A community meeting's been called at the Buddhist Church this evening. Everybody's in a flap—over nothing, I'm sure. But we'll go, if only to calm you down."

Mom's lip quivered. She hurried into the kitchen and threw together a hasty lunch. Kenny never did get his *haru maki*. Mom was too flustered to make them.

Kenny's first impression on walking into the Buddhist Church was that every Japanese person in Vancouver had crowded into the sanctuary and was talking at once. He could barely move in the crush of people. He heard clips from the conversations around him.

"Insane attack by Japan . . ."

"War in the Pacific . . ."

"What will Canada do?"

Dad stood with some men at one side of the room, while Mom went with Sally to sit on folding chairs that had been set up at the front for women, children and the elderly. Near them, Kenny spotted Mrs. Kimura, Dai's mother, and Mrs. Watanabe, Tak's mother. *It was funny*, he thought, *how the two women resembled their sons.* Mrs. Kimura was tall and skinny, plainly clothed in a dark blue dress. She had probing, intelligent black eyes; Kenny knew she had been a schoolteacher before Dai and his twin sisters were born. Mrs. Watanabe wore a deep purple silk dress, a fur coat over her arm. She was always decked out in heels and jewels. No surprise that Tak always wore the sharpest clothes and played with a new baseball glove every year.

As if the thought of Tak had conjured him up, Kenny spotted him, surrounded by his Clovers teammates, the group of them exuding an air of royalty. They all had to try out again, to keep their spots on the team, but everyone knew that, for Tak, at least, that was just a formality. He was a shoo-in.

Kenny turned away. *Where's Dai?* There he was, standing alone. Kenny waved, then squeezed through the bodies, dodging hips and shoulders, purses and babies, and met his friend in the middle.

"What a mob scene, eh?" Kenny shouted.

Dai scanned back and forth across the room. "I calculate there are . . . three hundred and eighty-five people here."

"Dai." Kenny rolled his eyes. Dai was probably right.

Nakata-sensei and Hashimoto-sensei, the monk who led the Buddhist congregation, mounted a platform and held up their hands for quiet. The noise slowly subsided.

"First, let us pray," Nakata-sensei said.

Hashimoto-sensei intoned a prayer in Japanese, asking for wisdom and peace, and then Nakata-sensei led the recitation of the Lord's Prayer. A hush fell over the room.

"We are gathered here to discuss the terrible events of the day," Nakata-sensei said, "and to determine what our community's response should be."

"Of course we condemn Japan," said one man, and there was a smattering of applause.

"And we should make that clear to the Canadian authorities," said Mr. Kimura, Dai's father.

"Yes . . . right," several people agreed.

Mr. Watanabe, Tak's father, strode to the front of the room. Kenny darted a look at Tak. The other boy was glancing around, as if making sure that people knew that that was *his* father. Mr. Watanabe was the publisher of the *Nikkei Clarion*, a popular Japanese language newspaper, and Tak was always bragging that his father had written this or that piece of news. Once, when he was younger, Kenny had said to Dad, "Mr. Watanabe must be a very important man, Dad."

"Why do you say that, Kenny?"

"Because Tak said he signed a treaty with Japan."

Dad had chuckled. "He's not *that* important, Kenny. Min Watanabe *writes* about the news, but he doesn't *make* the news."

Now, Mr. Watanabe bowed to the two religious leaders before turning to the crowd. "We can protest Japan's actions all we want, my friends, but that won't do any good. This attack means trouble for us."

"Trouble how, Mr. Watanabe?" Hashimoto-sensei asked.

"Because the government is going to blame us."

Blame us? Kenny thought. *Why us?*

"That's crazy!" someone said.

"Why would they, Min?" Kenny was surprised to hear Dad speak up. "They know we have nothing to do with the Japanese government. They know we're loyal Canadians."

"Is that why they won't let Nikkei into the armed forces?" Mr. Watanabe shot back.

"Well yes, that's true, but—" Dad began.

"Just you wait," Mr. Watanabe said. "Making us carry around identification cards as if we aren't even citizens is just the beginning. They'll accuse us of aiding the enemy and take away our rights as quick as you can blink."

Kenny was confused. What did Mr. Watanabe mean by *rights*? And why—how—would the government take them away?

"What are you afraid of, Min?" someone asked. "They'll take away our passports? Or lock us up?"

Several people laughed.

"That can't happen in Canada. It's a democracy, remember?" a woman said.

"With respect, Min, you're always crying gloom and doom," Dad said. "There's no reason to think that anything is going to happen to us. Sure, we are Nikkei, but we are Canadians first. I say, all we have to do is obey the law and everything'll be fine."

"Wishful thinking." Mr. Watanabe raised his finger. "Mark my words, our community is in for trouble. We have to stand strong and defiant—"

"No, no," other people said. "We mustn't make trouble."

"But we can't lie down and let them trample on us."

"No one's trampling! There's nothing to worry about."

Nakata-sensei and Hashimoto-sensei called for quiet.

"Mr. Watanabe's words may be correct, but nothing has happened to bear them out," Nakata-sensei said. "Let us stay calm. I believe Mr. Sakamoto is right. All we need to do is obey the law and show our loyalty, and we will be fine." He raised a hand. "Go in peace, and God bless you all."

That night, Dad came into Kenny's room to tuck him in.

"Dad?"

Dad put out the light, then turned in the doorway. "Yes?"

"What did Tak's father mean about taking our rights away?"

Dad came back and sat on the edge of Kenny's bed. Kenny sniffed his father's familiar smells of green tea and aftershave.

"Don't listen to that, Kenny. Min Watanabe is a cracker-jack newspaperman, but he's an agitator."

"What does that mean?"

Another pause. "Someone who tries to set things right."

"But that's good, isn't it?" Kenny asked.

"Yes, but he does it by stirring up trouble. He gets all riled up about things, and then he gets everybody else riled up. Don't worry about what he said."

"But if the government blames us—"

Dad put his hand on Kenny's shoulder. Kenny felt the warmth through his pajamas. "They're not going to. They know we have nothing to do with what Japan did. Don't give it a thought, Kenny."

Kenny looked at the outline of Dad's face in the dark. He could see where his bristly eyebrows stuck out, the outline of his jaw.

If Dad says it's okay, then it's okay. Japan is a long way away. Here, in Canada, in Vancouver, on Powell Street, everything is fine.

7

The next morning, as he lined up to enter his classroom, Kenny heard Tak talking to his pals. "You should have heard my father. He spoke out loud and clear. He said we should be strong." Tak glanced at Kenny. "Not like some people, who said we should just roll over like weaklings."

Kenny's face burned. Dad had not said they should roll over. He had said they should be good citizens. Kenny opened his mouth to reply, but just then the bell rang.

As he took his seat, Kenny noticed that Keith McAlary and Eddie Pavlich kept turning in his direction and whispering. Kenny had no idea what that was about, nor any time to wonder. He was too nervous. They were having an arithmetic test, and he was even worse at long division than he was at word problems.

Miss Morfitt handed a stack of papers to the first child

in every row. "Pass back the test and get your pencils out. Remember to show all your figuring."

Keith turned around and handed the stack to Kenny. At the top of the pile was a torn sheet of paper with scribbled words across it: DIRTY JAP SPY GO BACK WHERE YOU BELONG.

Kenny tried to stuff the paper into his pocket, but it was too late.

"Kenny?" Miss Morfitt said, coming down the aisle. "What's the problem?"

"Nothing, Miss Morfitt."

She stopped at his desk and held out her hand. Kenny gave her the paper.

"Where did this come from?"

"I don't know. It was . . . just on top."

The back of Keith's neck was red. Miss Morfitt took a step forward. "Keith, is this your work?"

He didn't answer.

"Keith?"

Miss Morfitt handed him the note. "Perhaps you'd like to share it with the class."

Keith snatched the paper. In a sullen voice, he read the words.

"Shut up, you creep!" Susana yelled.

"Susana!" Miss Morfitt said.

"Well, it's true," Keith said. "They *are* Japs, and the Japs attacked—"

"We do not use the word *Japs*," Miss Morfitt said sternly. She walked to the front of the classroom and folded her arms. Kenny expected her to yell, but instead she said in a quiet voice, "Kenny, where were you born?"

Surprised, he said, "Vancouver."

"Dai?"

"Victoria."

"Tak?"

"Steveston."

"Emiko?"

"Vancouver."

And so on through the class. Eighteen of the twenty-five students were of Japanese origin, and, with the exception of two who had recently arrived from Japan, all had been born in Canada.

Then Miss Morfitt began questioning the non-Japanese students. All but two had been born in Canada. Susana was one. When it was Keith's turn, he muttered, "Ireland."

Miss Morfitt nodded. "As you can see, almost all the children in this classroom were born here. They can't go *back* to Japan. They're Canadian.

"And as for spying," she went on, "that would be funny if it weren't so offensive. Can you imagine children in this classroom sending Canadian war secrets to Japan?"

There were titters of laughter. Keith flushed.

Miss Morfitt put up her hand. "That may be silly, but calling names is no laughing matter. I will not have it in my classroom. Ever. Is that clear?" She looked around the room.

"Yes, Miss Morfitt," the class chorused.

"That's better. Keith, go to the principal's office and wait for me there. The rest of you, start the test."

As Keith stood up, he turned and spoke quietly enough so that only Kenny could hear. "You're still a dirty Jap."

By the end of the day, though, Kenny felt better. At recess, all the white kids in the class, except for Keith and Eddie, had come up to their classmates and said, "Don't listen to those dumbbells." Kenny knew that Susana had orchestrated this, but it still felt good. Then, at midday, when he went home for lunch, Mom had made the *haru maki* especially for him. He went back to school with a bulging tummy.

Later, at Japanese language school, Nakata-sensei lifted a stack of slim books from a shelf. "Today we will begin to read the story of Momotaro. This will help you remember the vocabulary we have been learning. Now, who can tell me what *Momotaro* means?"

Naomi Tanaka raised her hand. "Little Peach Boy."

"Yes!" Nakata-sensei smiled. Kenny was glad for him. Hardly anyone ever knew the answers to Nakata-sensei's questions. And surely it would be more fun to read a story than to drill vocabulary words.

As the teacher started passing out the books, a knock sounded on the door. Nakata-sensei, along with the whole class, turned. A white man in a suit was standing there. He held what looked like a notice in his hand.

Nakata-sensei nodded. "Good afternoon, sir. How may I help you?"

The man strode into the room. His chin jutted out over the knot of his blue-and-red-striped tie. He held up the notice. Kenny could make out only one word: CLOSED, in heavy black type. "The Government of Canada has decreed that this school be closed until further notice."

Nakata-sensei froze, his arms full of books. "Excuse me? Closed?"

"Yes, all Japanese language schools and other institutions promoting Japanese language and culture are to be shut down."

"But—"

"I must insist that you vacate the premises immediately."

Kenny felt a surge of joy. *No more Japanese school! No more boring phrases. No more extra homework. Time to play or, maybe, practice baseball . . .* Some of the other children must have had the same idea, because he heard a few cheers.

But then he looked at Nakata-sensei's face. Tears rolled down his cheeks.

Their teacher was crying! Kenny had never seen this before.

"Surely you see, sir. These are children. They are no threat . . ."

The man took a step closer. "Canada is at war with Japan," he said in a hard voice. "All Japanese language instruction is banned. Now, will you vacate, or must I have you forcibly removed?"

The cheers and whispers ceased.

"No. I mean, yes, of course we will obey," Nakata-sensei said in a shaky voice. He turned to face the class, blinking rapidly. "Children, if you would please stand."

As if they had been given a silent instruction, all the children started helping to empty the room. Dai collected the storybooks that had just been passed out. Tak and a few others stacked up vocabulary workbooks. Emiko took down the illustrations of everyday objects, with their Japanese translations, that were tacked to the wall. Kenny and Naomi gathered the little rectangular boxes that held Nakata-sensei's inks and brushes.

Silently they filed out the door, onto the sidewalk. The younger class, some of the children crying, scampered out after them with their teacher. Sally darted to Kenny's side.

"Kenny," she said in a distressed voice.

Kenny took her hand.

The man nailed the notice to the door of the school. He fastened a heavy chain and padlock onto the door handles, pulling it taut to make sure it held. Then he left.

Kenny looked up at the pale, flat facade of the building, at the three arched windows over the front door. It was so silent. So empty.

Nakata-sensei turned to face the children. Fresh tears were rolling down his face. "I am sorry, children, please forgive me." He wiped his eyes. "You had better go home now."

He bowed to the children, and they bowed back.

That night, after dinner, Kenny quickly did his regular school homework, writing a sentence for each spelling word. Then he paged through his Japanese workbook, riffling past the empty pages. It felt strange not to have an assignment. For a moment, he actually missed it. His evening felt empty without those exercises, without the usual complaining thoughts. Inside his head he saw Nakata-sensei standing on the sidewalk, the tears on his cheeks. The padlock on the door.

The next day, Kenny walked Sally to her *odori* lesson. As usual, she had insisted on putting on her kimono and obi at home and parading through the streets in them. At least she had agreed to carry her geta and wear regular shoes for the walk—if she had insisted on wearing her wooden shoes, it would have taken even longer than the unbearably long time it did take, what with Sally greeting everyone with a flutter of her fan and admiring her reflection in every store window.

Finally they arrived at the studio. Kenny looked forward to dropping her off and having an hour to himself until he had to pick her up again. Today maybe he'd look at comic books at Tosa's Pharmacy. He had a little money in his pocket.

Mrs. Kobayashi was standing outside the door with her winter coat over her kimono. She had a strange look on her face.

"Good morning, Mrs. Kobayashi," Sally said politely. It always amazed Kenny how sweet she could be outside the house.

Mrs. Kobayashi bowed, but she didn't open the door.

"May I go in, please? I need to put on my geta," Sally said.

Suddenly Kenny knew what was coming. He put his hand on Sally's shoulder.

"I am sorry, Sally. There will be no lesson today. No more *odori* classes."

"Wh—how come?"

"The government will not allow it. No gatherings that promote Japanese culture."

Sally stood there, clutching the cloth bag that held her geta. "No more dancing?"

Mrs. Kobayashi shook her head.

It took a minute. Sally's mouth formed a round *O*. "But I want to dance! They can't do that!" She burst into tears.

"I am sorry, Sally." Mrs. Kobayashi blinked rapidly.

Sally sat down on the sidewalk and bawled into her hands. "It's not fair!"

"Come on, Sal," Kenny said. He got her to stand up. On the way home he stopped at Morita's Sweet Shop and bought her the biggest lollipop he could find.

8

Huddled under an umbrella, Kenny stamped his feet, trying to warm up. It was mid-December, nearly dark, and a chilly rain that sometimes turned into sleet, then into rain again, was falling.

He and his family were standing in a long line in front of the British Columbia Security Commission office. That morning, a notice had appeared in the newspaper: EFFECTIVE IMMEDIATELY, ALL PERSONS OF JAPANESE RACE ARE REQUIRED TO REGISTER WITH THE REGISTRAR OF ENEMY ALIENS.

Kenny couldn't figure that out. They weren't aliens. Dad had explained that an alien was someone who was not from the country. But they had all been born in Canada—well, all except Mom. She'd been born in Japan, but had become a naturalized Canadian citizen years ago.

And they weren't the enemy. Japan was the enemy. Germany was the enemy, and Italy. Not all these families living quietly in Vancouver. Not *his* family. Not *him*.

When they got inside, they were met by two men sitting at a table. One was an RCMP officer, his red serge jacket buttoned up tight. He looked familiar; Kenny recognized him as the older officer who had stopped them outside Woodward's. The other, a bald man with jowly cheeks and a red face, sat behind a sign that read REGISTRAR OF ENEMY ALIENS.

"Identity cards, please." The registrar put out his hand without looking at the Sakamotos.

Dad addressed him. "Sir, I think there is some mistake. We are not enemy aliens. What's more, I'm a veteran. Look, here's my voter registration card." Dad withdrew a card from his wallet and placed it on the table.

Kenny knew how proud Dad was of that card. Japanese Canadians were not allowed to vote, but after the Great War, Japanese veterans had petitioned the government to at least grant the vote to soldiers who had served their country. After a long struggle, the government had agreed.

At the last election, Dad had taken Kenny with him to the polling station. Dad had stood tall while a man inspected his voter registration card.

"Sakamoto, Hiroshi," the man had said, checking his name off a list. "Where did you serve?"

"France," Dad had answered.

"Belgium," the man said, and they'd shaken hands, smiling at one another.

Now, the registrar was not smiling. He didn't even look at Dad's voter registration card. "Sir, I won't ask again. Present your identity cards at once."

The RCMP officer added, "Do what the registrar says or I will remove you and your family." *He looks as if he hopes he'll have to*, Kenny thought.

"Harry," Mom said in a low voice.

Dad tucked his voter registration card back into his wallet and handed over his Japanese Canadian identity card. Mom and Mickey did the same. Dad passed over Kenny's and Sally's birth certificates.

Mom and Dad filled out forms. All five of them had their pictures taken and pressed their thumbs into an ink pad to make thumbprints. Kenny's hand felt greasy from the damp cloth he was given to wipe off the ink, and not all of it came off, so a black smudge remained on his finger.

Walking out of the office, Kenny looked at his card. REGISTRATION OF ENEMY ALIEN, it said over a picture of him. There were his chubby cheeks, the tuft of hair that always stuck up in the back. Was this the face of someone who could be an enemy to Canada?

What was worse was that he had a number. He was identified as 06247. Not just SAKAMOTO, KENJI, but a number. It made him feel as if part of him, his real, breathing, living self, had been taken away. That was how the registrar and the RCMP officer had looked at him—or, rather, not looked at him. He was just a Japanese. Nobody.

But I'm not, Kenny told himself. *I'm not an enemy. I'm not an alien. No matter what they say. No matter what it says on this card.*

But all the way home, the black on his thumb made him feel dirty. Not just on his hand. All over.

By the next morning, a brisk wind had blown the clouds away. The sky was a deep, clear blue. Across Burrard Inlet, the peaks gleamed with fresh snow.

"Let's go for a walk in Stanley Park," Dad said, and soon everyone was bundled up in scarves and mittens, Mom carrying a thermos of green tea.

They walked through downtown, past the darkened office buildings, past freighters in the harbor. Dad bought a bag of roasted chestnuts from a street vendor, and they munched on the warm, sweet nutmeats as they strolled. When they reached Stanley Park, they walked along the water, past Deadman's Island, around the peninsula, and headed northwest along Burrard Inlet. Here the mountains looked close enough to touch, but the family was in the shade now, and Kenny shivered, wishing he still had some hot chestnuts to keep him warm.

Mom pounced. "Kenny, you're chilled," she said. She found a bench and made him drink a cup of hot tea.

"Better?"

"Better."

By now it was mid-afternoon. Shadows were lengthening, and already the sun was nearing the horizon.

"Let's go see the memorial," Dad said.

Kenny didn't have to ask which one. *The memorial* meant only one thing.

They cut away from the water on a path leading into the heart of the park, and there it was. WORLD WAR I JAPANESE CANADIAN WAR MEMORIAL said a plaque at its base. Dad rubbed his fingers over the raised letters as if touching them could transport him back to the battlefields of France. Kenny had asked for the stories so many times he knew them by heart. How Dad had had to go to Alberta to enlist, since the British Columbia government would not accept Japanese volunteers. How, out of 190 Japanese Canadian soldiers, only 49 had returned home uninjured. How Dad had saved his captain's life by shooting a German sniper. How Dad's best friend, Stan, had died in his arms after being struck by an artillery shell, and how Dad had cried over his lifeless body. How the people of France had cheered the Japanese soldiers when they beat back the Germans, and toasted them with bottles of wine until, Dad said, "We thought we would float away."

Kenny let his eyes travel upward, following the graceful, fluted column of the obelisk as it rose into the sky, capped by a lantern with several tiny cutouts all around it and a miniature pagoda on top.

He must have noticed at the same moment that Dad did, because they both pointed.

"What's the matter?" Mom said, following their fingers.

"The light's not lit," Dad said. "It must have gone out. I'll have to find somebody and report it."

They walked back through the park and came upon a man wearing a badge that said STANLEY PARK RANGER.

"Excuse me, sir, I'd like to report a problem with the Japanese Canadian war memorial," Dad said.

"Yes, sir?"

"The light's gone out."

An uneasy look crossed the man's face. "Uh . . . there's no problem, sir. The light's been turned off."

There was a pause. "You mean, on purpose?"

"Yes."

"But the flame has been lit since 1920!"

The man flushed. "Orders from the federal government, sir. The light in the Japanese Canadian war memorial to be extinguished until further notice."

Dad stood there. At a slight tug of Mom's hand, he turned away.

They walked all the way back in silence. When they got home, Dad went straight to the dining room. He turned his photograph of the memorial around to face the wall.

That night, Kenny did something he had never done before. He sat his parents down and made them tea. When Mom protested and tried to help, he pushed her back into the living room. He heated the pot, as he'd seen Mom do a hundred times, and chose their favorite roasted green tea. He put two green tea cakes on a plate.

Dad took a sip, warming his hands on the cup. "Thank you, Kenji," he said. There were tears in his eyes. Kenny hurried back into the kitchen to clean up so he wouldn't have to see.

Weeks passed. The Japanese army rolled over Asia. In Kenny's neighborhood, people went about their business with worried expressions, as if wondering what would happen to them next. When asked by the police, they showed their enemy alien cards, then quickly stuffed them into their pockets or purses, as if they couldn't put them away fast enough.

In February, another notice appeared in the newspaper. EFFECTIVE IMMEDIATELY, JAPANESE CITIZENS ARE SUBJECT TO A CURFEW FROM DUSK TO DAWN.

When Dad read it out, Mickey's face turned red. "But . . . they can't do that! What about my Asahi team practice? We all have school, or jobs, so we can only meet at night."

Dad shrugged. "I'm sorry, Mickey."

Mickey stormed into their bedroom, and Kenny followed. "This is the most rotten thing ever!" Mickey exploded. "Now I can't meet the fellas at the gym. I can't keep up with my training. I can't stay in shape. And if I can't play baseball—" His voice broke off.

Kenny had no answer. Just the day before, he had walked home with Mickey from one of his Asahi team practices. The players had been talking about next season.

"I can't wait for baseball to start," Mickey had said. "I wish it was spring already."

"Bet you Fife is saying the same thing," one player had said. Then he'd imitated the other team in a silly voice. "'Let us at those Asahis. We'll show them this time.'"

"Think we can make it six championships in a row?" Mickey had asked.

"Sure, we can, with the 'nimble Nippon,'" another teammate answered, and the others had laughed.

"Aw, fellas," Mickey had said, but Kenny could tell that he enjoyed their teasing.

Now, Mickey took his baseball glove off the dresser and untied the string that kept it wrapped around a baseball— the ball from his winning hit the previous fall. He poured a little neatsfoot oil on the glove.

"I'll tell you one thing, Kenny. All this nonsense, the curfew and everything, had better be over before the season begins, or else," he said, rubbing the oil into the glove, massaging the palm and each finger until they glistened golden-brown. He looked up suddenly. "It will, won't it?"

"Gee, I don't know," Kenny said, surprised that Mickey was asking *him*.

"It's got to, Kenny! In all this crazy mess, baseball's the only thing that keeps me going."

"Sure, sure, Mickey," Kenny said quickly, alarmed at Mickey's tone. "It'll be fine by spring. Dad says the war in Asia'll be over real soon."

"Yeah," Mickey said, looking relieved. "Dad must be right. We'll beat Japan, and then we won't need the curfew anymore." He held out the glove, regarded it and rubbed one spot a little more. He replaced the ball in the palm and retied the glove. "The season will start as usual, and I'll be back with the fellas, and the Asahis will be stronger than ever. Right, Kenny?"

Kenny hesitated. Of course, he had no idea. But Mickey was staring at him with a desperate look on his face. "Right," he said.

Mickey nodded. "Yup. Just like normal." He replaced the glove on his dresser, gave it a little pat and left the room.

A nervous feeling fluttered in Kenny's stomach. He didn't like being the one doing the reassuring.

Several days later, at school, Kenny was surprised to see Tak standing by himself, arms folded across his chest. Tak's eyes were red, and when one of his buddies approached him, he snarled, "Leave me alone."

Kenny exchanged a confused look with Dai. The other boy shrugged. Miss Morfitt didn't say anything to the class, but Kenny noticed that she spoke to Tak in an extra-kind tone, and let him stay in at recess.

That evening, Kenny asked his parents what had happened. Mom started rubbing her thumbs together. Dad looked away. "You don't need to know, Kenny."

"Tell me."

Dad hesitated, then explained that the government had shut down all Japanese language newspapers.

"Including the *Nikkei Clarion*?" Kenny asked.

Dad nodded. "But Mr. Watanabe went ahead and printed his own newspaper, in defiance of the government's orders. He wrote an editorial detailing all the injustices against us, and distributed it secretly." Dad paused. "The government found out. Mr. Watanabe was arrested and sent to a prisoner-of-war camp in Ontario."

It took a moment to sink in. *Tak's father—arrested? Gone?* Kenny threw his arms around Dad. "That's not going to happen to you, is it?"

"Of course not," Dad said, stroking his back. "I'm not breaking the law. I'm not going anywhere."

"But . . . what will they do? Tak and his mother?"

"Mrs. Watanabe's family will help," Mom said.

A strange feeling rose in Kenny—sympathy for Tak. He thought for a moment. "That was brave, wasn't it?"

"Yes," Dad said. "Foolish, but brave."

After Kenny left the room, he heard Dad say, "I thought Min was out of his mind when he said those things at the meeting. But I have to admit he was right. They *are* cracking down on us."

"But, Harry—"

"Don't worry, Keiko. We're fine. I'm in no trouble. But . . . well, it's disturbing, that's all."

Kenny tiptoed to his room, a cold feeling in the pit of his stomach.

9

It was a sunny day in late February. Now that the days were getting longer, there was time to practice baseball before dark. Kenny had gone straight to the store after school to see if Mickey could get off work early and squeeze in a little training.

I really need to work on fielding, he thought.

Dad was showing a Minolta camera to a customer. "It's a twin-lens reflex, so what you see through the lens is exactly what you see on the film. Here, take a look . . ."

Kenny pulled Mickey aside. "Hey, Mickey, do you think we could—"

Raised voices outside caught his ear. He ran to the window. Uncle Jake was arguing with an RCMP officer. Kenny, Mickey and Dad rushed outside. The Mountie was plastering a notice on the window—right next to the one about the curfew and the one about the registration of enemy aliens and the one about the closure of Japanese language schools.

"This is how it started in Germany," Uncle Jake was shouting. "It's wrong. You can't do this."

The Mountie brushed glue over the notice. "I'm sorry, sir. Government orders."

Uncle Jake waved his arms. "These good people, you think they are going to take pictures of secret sites and send them to the enemy?"

"Sir, I'm asking you to stop—"

"It's discrimination, plain and simple—"

"Sir!"

Dad put his hand on Uncle Jake's shoulder. "Jake, let me see."

"Oh, Harry," Uncle Jake said sympathetically. He stepped aside.

Kenny slipped beside Dad and read the sign.

NO PERSON OF THE JAPANESE RACE MAY HAVE IN HIS POSSESSION ANY MOTOR VEHICLE, CAMERA, RADIO TRANSMITTER, RADIO RECEIVING SET, FIREARM, AMMUNITION OR EXPLOSIVE.

"No cameras!" Dad said.

"That's what I was trying to tell him," Uncle Jake said. "It's madness."

The officer picked up his pot of glue and addressed Dad. "That is correct, sir. You will have to take any cameras you own, plus any of these other items, to our downtown detachment."

Dad pointed at his store. "But . . . my business! My livelihood!"

"I'm sorry, sir. Government decree." The Mountie added, as if it provided any comfort, "You will be given a receipt, and these items will be held in trust until the cessation of hostilities."

"But . . . but . . ."

The Mountie, jaw clenched, turned and walked away.

Uncle Jake put an arm around Dad's shoulders. "I'm so sorry, Harry. I tried. He wouldn't listen. It's inhuman. Just like what happened to us."

Dad looked at him blankly.

"Do you want me to help you?"

"Help me?"

"Pack up."

The words seemed to jolt Dad out of his daze. "No. No, I have the boys. Thank you, though, Jake. I appreciate it."

Uncle Jake squeezed Dad's shoulder. He walked down the street.

Kenny and Mickey followed Dad back inside. The customer was gone. Dad slowly turned his head from side to side as if counting all his cameras, his lenses, his camera cases and photography books and frames. As if trying to gauge how much he was about to lose.

What are we going to do? Kenny thought in a panic. *How will we live? What if we have no money? Will we starve?* He thought of Tak and his mother, without an income. He'd never thought it would happen to *him*.

And, he thought, his mind racing, *does this mean there won't be enough money for a Clovers uniform? Or a new glove?*

Instantly he felt guilty. It wasn't right to be thinking about himself now.

"Mickey—" Dad's voice cracked. He started again. "Mickey, go in the back room and fetch as many boxes as you can find. Kenny, you make a list."

They set to work. Dad took each camera and read out the make and model. Kenny wrote down the information. Dad lovingly wrapped the camera in cotton batting, and Mickey laid it in a box. When the box was full, Mickey sealed it with tape, and they started on a new box.

One time Dad paused, cradling a camera in his hands. "I remember when I got this Kodak in. The first flash camera!" Another time, holding a lens, he said, "I shot the heron with this," glancing at his photo on the wall. Kenny followed his gaze. The bird's shiny eye seemed to be glinting straight at him.

Dad's face fell. He went back to packing.

The boxes piled up by the front door. Kenny filled page after page. The shelves and display cases and front window emptied out.

Finally Mickey sealed the last box. He and Dad stacked the boxes on a dolly. Kenny opened the door so they could roll it out, but Dad said, "Wait." He turned back and walked around his empty store, pausing in front of each of his photos. The heron. His war medal. The baseball game at the Powell Street Grounds. The fishermen and their nets.

"I built this store from scratch," he whispered. "I was so proud, and I—" His voice broke off.

He left the photos on the walls. He flipped the OPEN sign over to CLOSED. Then he wheeled the dolly out the door and headed to the RCMP station.

Kenny didn't think it could get any worse. But a month later, it did. A lot worse.

A new bulletin had appeared: ALL MALES OF THE JAPANESE RACE BETWEEN THE AGES OF EIGHTEEN AND FORTY-FIVE ARE TO BE REMOVED FROM A ONE-HUNDRED-MILE-WIDE "SECURE ZONE" ALONG THE WEST COAST OF BRITISH COLUMBIA.

The notice said that they would be sent to road camps in the interior, or in other provinces, to build roads or perform other labor. SAKAMOTO, HIROSHI, 06773 appeared on a list of men to be sent to a road camp outside Revelstoke, four hundred miles away in the mountains.

At first, Kenny refused to believe it. It wasn't possible that Dad would be sent away, that he, Mom, Mickey and Sally would be left on their own. *It's not real, it's not real*, he told himself. But the days had ticked by, and now, in March, he and his family were standing on the Canadian Pacific Railway platform, Dad in a neatly ironed suit and hat, his suitcase at his feet.

All around Kenny, family groups huddled together. Men clutched suitcases. Children clung to their fathers' hands, staring in awe at the huge black locomotive steaming on the track, belching clouds of smoke. Everywhere, Kenny saw stony faces, people struggling not to cry. A few furtively wiped away tears.

Kenny looked at the other families and he saw their sadness. But he didn't feel sad. He felt numb, disbelieving. It wasn't possible that in a few minutes Dad would get on that train and be gone.

An RCMP officer came along and checked Dad's name off a list. A bullhorn blared. Mom jumped. "All Japanese road camp inmates must now board the train."

Dad picked Sally up, and she threw her arms around him. "Oh, Daddy, don't go!"

"Now, Sally, none of that. You be a good girl and mind Mommy, all right?"

Sally nodded a tear-stained face.

Dad put her down, then held Kenny by both arms. "You, too, Kenny. Be a good boy—I know you will. Help Mom. But don't overdo it. Be careful. Take it easy."

The sadness hit, finally, suddenly. *Dad! Oh, Dad!* Kenny's throat felt thick. He wanted to grab Dad and not let go.

How will we manage? What will we do without Dad to answer questions, to make rules? To reassure us? To keep us on track? To be a family?

He didn't grab. He didn't cry. He managed to nod, breathing in his father's smells of green tea and aftershave.

Dad put his hand on Mickey's shoulder. "My son—"
His voice choked. "You are the man of the house. Look
after your mother and your brother and sister."

"But, Dad, I don't know how—"

Dad put his finger to Mickey's lips. "You can. I know I
can count on you."

Mickey nodded, a frightened look in his eyes.

Finally Dad enfolded Mom in his arms.

"Oh, Harry, what will I do without you?"

Dad lowered his head onto her shoulder. He spoke in a
low voice. He was speaking Japanese, but Kenny could
make out that he was telling her that she had to be brave,
that Mickey would take care of her, that Auntie Miriam
and Uncle Jake would help. Mom nodded. She stepped
away, her face a mask. A mask with glistening eyes.

Dad stood tall. He picked up his suitcase and climbed
the iron steps onto the train.

Without speaking, Kenny, Mickey, Sally and Mom
moved closer together. The train whistle blew, three sharp
blasts. A gust of steam was released. The wheels began to
roll, slowly, then faster. The long black train moved down
the track. In car after car, Kenny saw men's faces pressed
against the windows. Then they disappeared.

10

The next few weeks were dreary. During the day, Mom cooked and cleaned as usual, but at night, Kenny heard her crying. Her body seemed deflated, like a gourd whose insides have been hollowed out.

Kenny went to school. He did his homework. But his mind was somewhere else, following Dad's train. The best part of his day was walking to and from school with Susana. She didn't pester him with questions about whether he missed Dad or if he was sad. She didn't have to. She knew. Kenny appreciated her silence. It was more comforting than any cheerful chatter would have been.

Sally followed Mom around like a shadow. Sometimes she even held on to Mom's skirt, like a toddler. When Mom told her to do something, make her bed or bring in the milk bottles, she whined, "I don't want to," and Mom didn't even scold her, she just sighed. Kenny had to say,

"Sally, do it." Then Sally sniffed, glaring at him—but she did it.

Mickey went to school, came home, did chores. He carried groceries up the stairs. He lugged the basket of clothes from the wringer washer to the clothesline on the balcony. He went to the bank and withdrew money; Dad had put his name on the account and showed him how to fill out the slips.

Mickey did all this, but Kenny saw that he went around with his jaw clenched and a dark look in his eyes. He slammed doors. He lay on his bed, face to the wall.

One day a pile of bills arrived in the mail. Mickey sorted through them. He looked from one envelope to another. Then he swept all the papers off the table, standing up so abruptly that his chair toppled over backward with a crash.

"I can't do this! I don't know how! It's not fair!"

"Mickey, please," Mom begged, glancing at the open window. She rubbed her thumbs together. "Don't make trouble. Someone might hear, and who knows what might happen."

Mickey colored. He picked up the chair, gripping the wooden back, his knuckles white. "I'm sorry, Mom. Forgive me." He went back to the bills.

Later, when Kenny and Mickey were getting ready for bed, Kenny put a hand on his brother's shoulder.

Mickey stood in the middle of the room. He turned slowly, scanning the pictures on the walls, pausing at each Asahi player, all the way around. He gave a strained smile. "Baseball'll start soon, Kenny. That'll make everything okay."

A few weeks later, a letter arrived from Dad. Kenny's heart leaped to see the familiar handwriting.

April 7, 1942
My dearest ones,

We are living in tents while some of the men quickly throw up bunkhouses. There is still snow on the ground in the high places. It is cold in the tents. The food is ▓▓▓▓▓▓▓▓▓▓▓▓▓▓▓▓ no rice or shoyu. We work ▓▓▓▓▓▓▓▓▓▓▓▓▓▓ till dusk. I miss you. Be well.

Your loving husband and father,
Hiroshi

Eyes wet, Mom held the letter to her chest.

Kenny wondered what Dad wasn't saying. *Does his back ache from the hard work? Are his hands, always so clean, now dirty and rough? Does he, too, cry at night, missing Mom?*

And when will we see him again?

Soon after, a different letter arrived, an official-looking one. It was from the British Columbia Security Commission, and it was addressed to SAKAMOTO, MRS. KEIKO, 06776.

Mom started reading. She looked up, bewildered. "I don't understand."

Kenny took the letter from her. The heading said EVACUATION OF ALL JAPANESE. He read aloud: "By decree of the Government of Canada, all persons of Japanese origin will be evacuated from the one-hundred-mile-wide 'secure zone' along the West coast of British Columbia and moved to internment camps in the interior."

"But . . . that's us," Mom said, sounding dazed.

The letter fell from Kenny's hand. "We have to leave? Where . . . ? How . . . ? Is it . . . forever?"

"I—I don't know," Mom said. She started crying.

That alarmed Kenny more than anything. Mom hadn't cried in front of them, not even when Dad left.

As if on cue, Sally started wailing. "Mommy! Mommy!"

"Let me see that," Mickey said. He snatched up the letter. His hand shook. "I'm not going."

Mom put her hand on his arm. "Hush, Mickey! Don't talk like that."

He shook off her hand, a wild look in his eyes. "I don't care. I'll find my friends. We'll stay. We'll hide. We'll play ball. I don't care if there's no one in the stands, as long as I can play—"

He ran out of the house.

"Mickey! Oh God, he'll get in trouble." She ran down the stairs after him. Kenny and Sally followed. Mom looked left and right. There was no sign of Mickey.

"He'll come back, Mom," Kenny said. He hoped he was right. Surely Mickey wouldn't do anything stupid.

On the street, neighbors were standing with letters in their hands, looking around vacantly.

"What does it mean?"

"Where will we go?"

"How will we live?"

No one had answers.

Mom joined a group of women clustered at the corner, and Kenny shuffled closer to hear. "How will we fit under the limit?" one woman was saying.

"What limit?" Mom asked.

The woman showed her in the letter where it said that adults would be allowed to take one hundred and fifty pounds of belongings; children, seventy-five pounds. All of their other possessions—their homes, their furniture, everything—would be held by the Custodian of Enemy Alien Property.

Kenny hadn't read that far.

"One hundred and fifty pounds!" Mom said. "Why, my dishes and cookware must weigh that much."

"That's why it's impossible. We have to pack warm clothes and bedding and food. Everything to live on . . ."

"For who knows how long," another woman added.

"But what about everything else?" Mom asked. "Keepsakes, jewelry, photographs . . ."

The women shrugged. One said she planned to leave those things boxed up in her home. Another woman said she didn't trust the authorities not to go through her house. She was going to bury her most precious things in the backyard. A third woman shook her head. "I'm going to sell my things and take the money—because who knows if we'll ever get our homes back?"

Mom's eyes filled. Her thumbs rubbed back and forth.

"At least we get to stay in our homes until they ship us out," the first woman said bitterly. "Some people are being held at Hastings Park until they get sent away. They're sleeping in cattle pens."

Cattle pens? Kenny thought. *Like animals?*

"This government has no conscience," one woman said angrily.

Just then, an RCMP officer walked down the street. He waved his nightstick. "Go along, now, back to your homes. No gatherings of Japanese. Go on."

Kenny took Mom and Sally by the hand and led them inside. Mom started collecting things. Dishes and coats, jewelry and nightgowns, teapots and shoes. She heaped them in the living room. Then she collapsed on the couch. "What do I do? I don't know what to do."

Kenny did the only thing he could think of. He ran for Auntie Miriam.

After she returned with Kenny and read the letter, she enfolded Mom in her arms. "Oh, Keiko."

Mom sniffled.

Auntie Miriam shook her head. "When Jake and I came here, to Canada, we thought we had come to paradise. A land of justice, a land of fairness. But now—I am ashamed. Ashamed of my own government."

Mom dried her eyes. "Oh, Miriam, what do I take? What do I leave? And what do I do with my precious things?" She knelt down and pointed from one pile to the next. "My pinecone dishes. I brought them from Japan for my wedding, each one wrapped in rice paper, and not one broke! Harry's beautiful framed pictures. My jewelry, handed down from my *obaasan*. My kimonos. Letters from my family . . ." Her voice trailed off.

Auntie Miriam took Mom's hand. "Now, you leave that to me. Jake and I will keep it all safe for you, I promise. We'll store it for you until this wretched war is over and you come home again."

"Thank you," Mom said, her voice trembling.

"Let's start with what you'll take," Auntie Miriam said.

Mom took a deep breath. She set her jaw. "Okay." She and Auntie Miriam and Kenny got to work. One trunk with Mom's warm clothes for the cold interior winters, plus blankets and pillows for the family, her sewing basket.

Another trunk with cooking pots, rice bowls, chopsticks, flagons and cups, cooking tools. A wooden box with food: sacks of rice, sugar and salt, sheets of nori, bottles of shoyu and vinegar, cans of salmon and beans.

Then they tackled the things Mom was going to leave behind. They wrapped them in paper or silk and packed them in boxes. Several times Mom paused, fluttering a lacquered fan, sniffing a packet of letters, holding a gold earring up to the light, turning it this way and that. Each time, a look came over her face, and Kenny thought she was going to cry. But each time, she composed herself, moving on to the next thing, and the next.

After several boxes had been packed, Kenny heard footsteps on the stairs. He and Mom exchanged a look. Mickey came in. Kenny braced himself, but Mickey was calm. His eyes were downcast.

He bowed. "I am sorry," he said in a low voice. "I was—I don't know what I was thinking. Let me help."

Mom put her hand on his shoulder.

Mickey started packing.

When the boxes of keepsakes were filled up, Mickey and Uncle Jake carried them down the Sakamotos' front stairs, up the Bernsteins' front stairs, and then up another flight of stairs to their attic. At first, Mickey wouldn't let Kenny help, but after the fourth trip, wiping the sweat from his brow, he relented and let Kenny carry the smaller, lighter boxes.

Susana met Kenny at the door. Her eyes were red. "I don't want you to go," she said in a low voice.

"Me neither." Kenny hid his face behind the box he was carrying. *It's not fair and I'm afraid I'll never see you again and I'm scared of where we're going and how can I possibly get on without you?* he wanted to say. But he didn't. Because if he said one more word, he knew he would start blubbering and never stop.

"Now," Mom said to Kenny and Mickey when they came back, "I'll start packing for Sally. You two go pack your own things. Remember, the winters are cold in the interior, so take your warmest clothes. And boots. And hats and mitts. And try to find clothes that are big on you, so you can grow into them."

For Kenny, that part was easy. Clothes were clothes, and who cared how they looked? He picked out woolen sweaters and flannel pajamas, woolen trousers, blue jeans and long-sleeved shirts. His winter coat, hat, mittens and boots. A bathing suit, some shorts and T-shirts, because surely it couldn't be cold all the time there—wherever *there* was. He stuffed them into a suitcase.

But what about all his other things, the important things, which couldn't be packed? His bed, his room, his house. The way the lamplight fell over his pillow just right. The comforting sound of Mom and Dad murmuring in the next room. Walking to school with Susana. Everything he knew, everywhere he felt at home. His life. Gone. And to what? What lay ahead?

Kenny squeezed his eyes shut and clenched his fists. He breathed deeply. He would not cry. He would not. More deep breaths. There. The tears were gone.

Then he noticed that Mickey was just sitting on the edge of his bed, elbows on knees, head hanging down. He had thrown a bunch of clothes into his suitcase, which lay open on the floor.

"Mickey! Aren't you going to take your Asahi uniform?"

Mickey shook his head. "What's the point? I'll never wear it again."

"What do you mean?"

"There isn't going to be a season. Who knows if there will ever be one again?"

"But—"

"Everything. Over. Ruined. And right when I was—" Mickey swallowed. "—Rookie of the Year," he said bitterly. "The Asahis are finished. And so am I." One by one he tore down the Asahi pictures from the walls. Then he left the room.

No! Kenny thought. *The Asahis over? It can't be.*

Then a thought hit him. He grabbed a calendar. He put his finger on today's date in May and traced back . . . back . . . April . . . March . . .

He sat there, stunned. The date for the tryouts had come and gone. They hadn't happened. No tryouts for the Clovers, or the Beavers or the Athletics. Or the Asahis. In the confusion of the last few weeks, he'd forgotten all about it.

Mickey's right. This really is the end of the Asahi baseball club, and all the junior teams, too. I'll never get to try out for the Clovers. Never be able to dream of rising through the ranks to the Asahis. Never wear one of those uniforms.

Kenny lay down and curled into a ball. He bawled.

In a secret place inside himself, he was relieved. He really had no chance of making the team anyway, so now he was spared the humiliation of making a fool of himself.

Of trying and being rejected. Of hearing the other kids whisper, "What was that dopey Kenny Sakamoto thinking? Him, on the Clovers? Forget it."

But the relief was swallowed by a deep ache. Now Dad would never cheer for him when he came up to the plate, would never say, "My son, Kenny, the Asahi," would never look at him the way he looked at Mickey.

Kenny pressed his face into his pillow. He cried until he had no more tears. Then he slowly sat up. His head felt thick. His throat hurt.

He looked at his baseball glove, sitting on the dresser. A fine layer of dust coated it, so little had it been used in the past weeks.

Still, Kenny couldn't leave it behind, even if it only served to remind him of what he had dreamed of, what he had lost. He put it into his suitcase.

Then he looked at Mickey's Asahi uniform, hanging in the closet.

Kenny squeezed Mickey's uniform, cleats, cap and glove into his brother's suitcase. There was no point, he knew. There might not ever be another Asahi game. But he couldn't leave Mickey's uniform behind. Mickey might not know it, but that uniform had to come.

11

The train platform was a mass of people on this bright June morning, women clutching baskets of food, old people sitting on their suitcases or leaning on their canes, babies crying, some children standing stiffly next to their mothers, others playing tag, darting around the porters. A hubbub of Japanese and English, questions and answers, scoldings and good-byes, filled the air.

A few days earlier, in church, Nakata-sensei had told the congregation that he and his family were being sent to a place called New Denver.

"There is a United Church there," Nakata-sensei had said, "and the minister is doing all he can to welcome us. Men from a local road camp are building shacks for Japanese families right now. I don't know what the living conditions will be like, but if some of you join us, at least we will have a church community."

That announcement was just the thing Mom needed to make up her mind. The government had been pressing families to decide which camp to go to. She would follow Nakata-sensei.

When they had arrived home from church, they looked at a map. New Denver was a tiny dot on the eastern shore of a long lake called Slocan Lake. Kenny's finger had traced a line northward. "Look, Mom." New Denver wasn't that far from Revelstoke—on the map, anyway. Maybe they'd get to see Dad.

In the flurry of getting ready, Kenny's tenth birthday on June 7 had come and gone. Mom had made him *haru maki* and *manjū* cakes, but there had been no party, no celebration.

"I'm sorry, Kenny," Mom had said that night, tucking him in.

"That's okay, Mom. I understand," he'd said. And he did. *Who feels like celebrating when you're preparing to leave your home and everything you know?*

Now, they stood on the platform. Kenny chafed in his dress-up shirt. "Why do we have to wear nice clothes to be sent away?" he'd asked Mom that morning. She'd put on a gray linen suit, and Mickey was in a sports jacket and tie.

"To look proper and presentable," she'd answered.

Kenny knew not to argue.

Piled at their feet was everything that they were allowed to take: Mom's two trunks, the box of food, and a suitcase each for Kenny, Sally and Mickey. Plus a basket of food for the journey, which, they had been told, would take nearly two days: a thermos of tea, boiled eggs, rice balls wrapped in nori, cucumber pickles, *kakimochi*—the fried crackers coated with sugar and shoyu, which Sally especially loved. And a bag of rugelach from Auntie Miriam.

It had been painful, saying good-bye to the Bernsteins. They had come over late the night before, after the last-minute packing was done. Uncle Jake and Auntie Miriam had repeated their promise to look after Mom's things. "And we'll keep an eye on your house, too," Uncle Jake had pledged.

A line of tears had trickled down Mom's cheeks when Uncle Jake and Auntie Miriam hugged her. Sally and Gittie had sobbed in each other's arms. Even Mickey had sniffled when he shook their hands.

Kenny and Susana had found a quiet corner. They sat side by side on the floor, knees bent, not looking at each other.

"It's rotten," Susana said.

"Yeah." Kenny's throat was thick.

A pause. "I know what it's like to leave your home. It's awful." Her voice trembled.

Kenny didn't answer.

"But you do meet great friends," Susana added.

"I won't meet anyone like you. Ever."

Another silence. Kenny heard a sniffle. He swallowed several times.

"You'll be fine," Susana said in a fake-cheerful voice.

"I know. So will you."

"Yeah, with the likes of Maggie Resnick, playing dolls." She snorted. The snort turned into a sob.

Kenny's eyes filled. He blinked rapidly. "I'll write—if they let us."

"I will, too."

"Don't let Keith McAlary and Eddie Pavlich push you around."

"You bet I won't."

They sat in silence, knees touching.

Now, Kenny teared up, thinking of all the things he wished he'd told her. That she was brave. That she was a great roller-skater. That she was the best best-friend ever.

Wiping his eyes, he peered down the track, trying to see how far the train went. He counted twelve cars and still couldn't see the end of them. He had never seen such a long train.

Then he saw something else. Or, rather, someone. Tak Watanabe and his mother. Tak stood with arms crossed, a sullen look on his face. Mrs. Watanabe, jewels sparkling at her ears, clutched her purse to her chest. She wore a fancy pale blue spring coat with a fox fur collar. Her back was as straight as a fence post. She had been a famous *odori* dancer. Kenny remembered seeing her perform. He remembered how graceful she was.

Kenny wondered how they still managed to look so well off. His own family had had to watch every penny since Dad's store had been closed, and none of them had purchased anything new in months. Tak didn't show signs of wanting for anything. He still dressed well, still had the newest running shoes, the best baseball glove.

Baseball, Kenny thought, and realized something. Tak hadn't been able to try out for the Clovers either. And, unlike Kenny, he would have made the team again for sure. So this was a real loss for him.

And that wasn't the worst thing. The worst thing was

what had happened to his father. As bad as it was to have Dad in a work camp in Revelstoke, it was worse to have your father in a prisoner-of-war camp in Ontario and not know when, or if, he would get out.

But feeling sorry for Tak didn't make Kenny like him. *Please don't put us together in the same camp*, he thought.

A whistle blew. Kenny jumped. The doors to the train cars slid open.

"All aboard!" a voice commanded through a bullhorn.

People jostled, dragging and lifting suitcases, passing babies from one set of arms to another, squeezing past each other in the crowded cars, bowing and murmuring apologies.

Kenny took Sally's hand while Mickey held Mom's elbow. Somehow they found seats together, facing one another. The trunks went into a baggage compartment. Mickey hoisted the suitcases onto the overhead rack. There wasn't room for everything, so the wooden box went under Sally's feet. Mom held the food basket on her lap. The train car filled with the aromas of pickles and hard-boiled eggs, the sounds of nose-blowing and words of comfort.

The doors closed. The train whistle blew, three sharp blasts, just as it had when Dad left. Kenny felt the train car jolt backward, banging against the car to its rear, then begin to slide forward, slowly, slowly. In spite of himself—in spite of the look of terror on Mom's face and the look of misery on Mickey's, in spite of the knot in his stomach about where they were going and what would happen and how Dad was and when they would see him and how they would live— he felt a shiver of excitement. This was his first train ride, ever, and the sound of the wheels and the smell of the smoke and the prickly plush of the seats and the smart blue and red uniforms of the conductors were all thrilling.

The train picked up speed. Kenny leaned forward to see past Sally. As the huge stone train station vanished, and the buildings of downtown appeared and disappeared, in a flash, in a blur, his heart gave a rapid little stutter, and he could almost imagine that they were setting off on a grand adventure.

12

It wasn't. After one-and-a-half boring days on the train to Nelson, then a long bus ride to New Denver up a winding road along a river with steep mountains rising on either side, Kenny was stiff, dusty, sweaty and exhausted.

As the bus rumbled through town, he peered through the window at this village that was to be their new home. It was tiny, just half a dozen streets wide. He spotted a couple of grocery stores, a hardware store, a bank, a drugstore, a government building, a hotel. There were no traffic lights. No buses or streetcars. No movie theaters.

The bus stopped in front of an old ice arena, and the passengers filed off. Several townspeople clustered nearby, gawking at them. One woman, pushing a baby carriage, crossed the street, making a wide berth around them, then crossed back.

"Look at those Chinks," a little boy said.

"They're not Chinks, stupid, they're Japs," a girl answered.

The Japanese stared resolutely ahead.

"What's the difference? They all got black hair and slit eyes." The boy pulled the skin around his eyes toward his ears and started hopping around.

The other children laughed and joined the game. "Slit eyes, slit eyes . . ."

Around him Kenny heard murmurs, other voices hushing them. Mickey took a step toward the children, but Mom pulled him back. "Mickey, don't!"

Kenny could see Mickey shaking, but he stayed put.

An official barked at Kenny's family and several others to climb up into the back of a truck. It had high wooden slats around the bed, as if to hold in cattle. They bounced a few miles down the same road they'd just driven up in the bus, across a raging creek—a sign said CARPENTER CREEK—and pulled onto a dirt road leading to what looked like a farm. Only there were no crops, no animals, no barns. Fresh stumps showed where trees had recently been cut down, with tall meadow grass, mostly trampled, between them. Kenny heard someone say that this place was called the Orchard, so he supposed that the cut-down trees had been fruit trees.

Trucks relayed back and forth from town, dropping passengers and their luggage. Soon there were about a hundred people clustered in the meadow.

Down the hill from where he was standing, Kenny could see a blue-gray sheen of water, which he knew was Slocan Lake. On the far shore, a massive mountain rose, its forested slopes topped by a jagged, snow-covered peak. It was beautiful, in a stark, forbidding way, but right now Kenny wasn't appreciating its beauty. All around him, babies wailed and little kids whined and old people leaned on their children, looking ready to fall over. He felt the same, and sat down on his suitcase.

Sally had reverted, on the trip, to sucking her thumb, something she hadn't done since she was three, and she absently rubbed her index finger across her nose as she sucked, removing her thumb only long enough to whine to Mom that she wanted to go to sleep, in her bed, *now*, and then sticking it back in. Mom looked as if she were going to cry. And Mickey—Mickey had barely said a word since they'd boarded the train. He'd sat with his arms folded and his jaw clenched, getting up only to help Mom unpack the food basket or take Sally to the bathroom, then folded back in on himself, glowering from under his hooded eyelids. Even now he stood slightly apart from the rest of the family, fists clenched.

On the slope of the Orchard, Japanese men were building small buildings, wood-framed with shake roofs. The noise was constant: hammering and sawing, shouting in English and Japanese, a parade of laborers carrying boards, sacks of nails, bundles of shakes. Sawdust flew. About a dozen shacks were already built, and three or four more were in various stages of completion. Each had a number painted in yellow on its front. Kenny remembered Nakata-sensei saying that homes were being built for the families, but surely these tiny shacks couldn't be those. *I wonder what they're for. Storage, maybe?*

Two white men walked toward the group of Japanese. The younger of the two was an RCMP officer, wearing the usual red serge and peaked hat. The other, a skinny man with pomaded brown hair and a harassed expression, was dressed in a suit. He blew a whistle, and the crowd quieted down.

"My name is Harley Richardson, and I am with the British Columbia Security Commission. I am the supervisor of this internment camp. This is my colleague, Constable Daniel Murphy. He will help me keep the peace."

Mr. Richardson glared at the crowd as if he expected violations of the peace at any moment. Constable Murphy lifted his hat and nodded.

"Listen for your cabin assignments," Mr. Richardson shouted. "When I call your name, take your belongings and go to your cabin. There will be two families per cabin." He gestured down the hill, and Kenny realized with a shock that those shacks *were* the cabins. Not storage sheds. The Japanese were going to have to live in them. But they were so small. Two families? Impossible!

Mr. Richardson lifted a clipboard. "Cabin number one—"

"Excuse me, sir?"

Kenny turned. An elderly man had raised his hand.

"Yes?" Mr. Richardson snapped.

"Yes, thank you, sir, but there don't seem to be enough cabins for everyone."

Mr. Richardson's face turned red. "I'm aware of that. Some families will have to live in tents. Temporarily."

"Tents!" A volley of comments in English and Japanese rippled through the crowd.

Mr. Richardson waved his arms. "It's not my fault. We weren't given enough notice, or enough manpower. We're building shacks as fast as we can."

There was another ripple of dismay.

Please let us get a shack, Kenny thought. It was selfish, but right now he didn't care. Even one of those tiny shacks would be better than a tent.

"Attention!" Mr. Richardson yelled, and blew his whistle again. He consulted the clipboard. "Cabin number one. Nishihara family and Kitiwaga family. Cabin number two . . ."

The families began to move. Kenny knew the Kitiwaga family from down the street. Elderly Mr. and Mrs. Kitiwaga linked arms and tottered down the path. Their daughter-in-law, Eiko, wedged one suitcase under each arm and then lifted two more, one in each hand. She took a few steps. The two suitcases under her arms slipped. Her face red and sweaty, she set down the two in her hands and wedged in the other two again. Again they slipped. Kenny saw tears roll down her cheeks. An older man stepped forward and picked up two of the suitcases. Eiko bowed to him, wiping her eyes.

"Cabin number six, Kimura family . . ."

Dai!

Kenny hadn't seen him on the train or bus, or in the crowd in New Denver, or here. But there he was, with his mother, his twin sisters and his grandparents. For a moment, Kenny's heart lifted, so happy was he to see his classmate. As Dai shuffled past, his skinny arms wrapped around a large, heavy-looking wooden box, his eye caught Kenny's, and he, too, started in surprise. They smiled at one another.

"Cabin number nine . . ."

The crowd thinned. The remaining families gathered closer together.

"Cabin number twelve, Sakamoto family . . ."

Kenny shot up.

Who would the other family be? Someone nice, he hoped, with a boy his age. Someone who'd want to play with him . . .

"And the Watanabe family."

No.

Maybe there were some other Watanabes, ones whom Kenny had never met. *Please*, he prayed, *not Tak.*

Tak and his mother stepped forward. Mrs. Watanabe clutched her purse to her chest. Her fancy coat was dusty and creased, the fox's fur drooping around her neck. She began to step carefully toward the cabins. Tak lifted one large suitcase and dragged a trunk along the ground. As he passed Kenny, he averted his eyes.

"Come, Sally," Mom said, taking her hand and Sally's suitcase in the other.

Sally's thumb popped out of her mouth, and a wail flew out after it. "I can't walk anymore, Mommy. I can't!"

"Now, Sally—"

Sally burst into tears. Mom looked helplessly at Mickey, who had hoisted one of the trunks on his shoulder and gripped the handle of the other.

"Leave Sally's suitcase, Mom," he muttered. "I'll go back."

With a sniffle, Sally jumped into Mom's arms. Kenny lifted his and Sally's suitcases, but then put Sally's down. He needed two hands for his own. He would go back with Mickey and carry the remaining two.

His suitcase banging against his legs with each step, Kenny followed Mom and Sally down a dirt path that wound past several other shacks. Suitcases, trunks and boxes were piled outside them. From inside some of the shacks came dismayed and angry voices; from others, silence.

Several times Mickey had to stop and rearrange the trunks, switching shoulders and hands. Each time, Mom paused, waiting for him, her face turning red with the strain of carrying Sally. Finally Mickey said, "Go on, Mom."

Mom nodded, and she and Kenny staggered on. Past cabin number ten, cabin number eleven . . .

Tak and Mrs. Watanabe were standing outside the door. The shack was long and narrow. Yellow trails dripped from the painted *1* and *2* on the front wall.

Mom and Mrs. Watanabe bowed.

"Mrs. Sakamoto."

"Mrs. Watanabe."

Kenny forced himself to say, "Tak."

"Kenny."

"And this is Sally," Mom said.

They stood there. *No one wants to be the first to go in and see how bad it is*, Kenny thought.

Mrs. Watanabe gestured with her hand, and Mom stepped inside. The others followed. They crowded together just inside the door.

It was worse than Kenny could have imagined. They were in a small square room. The walls were bare wooden boards. An iron cookstove stood against the wall to his left. Jutting out from the back wall was a wooden sink, whose drainpipe looked like it emptied onto the ground beneath the floor. A pot-bellied stove sat in the near corner. Above it, mounted to the wall, was a contraption with a metal bottom and a fluted glass top. Another one was mounted above the sink. Kenny stared at them for a moment. What could they be? Then it came to him. Kerosene lamps. *That means there's no electricity.* He looked around, searching for wires, outlets. Nothing.

No toilet either.

Two smaller rooms were built on either side of the central room. Each one was equipped with a wooden bed frame under a canvas-covered mattress about an inch thick, and a small wooden stool.

That was it.

Kenny realized that he, Mom, Mickey and Sally were going to have to share that tiny bedroom.

That was bad. But it wasn't the worst thing. The worst thing was that he was going to have to live in this place with Tak.

Mrs. Watanabe gave a cry and sank onto a small stool beside the door. While Mom looked around in confusion, Sally ran to the bed in the room on the left, curled into a ball and stuck her thumb in her mouth.

Kenny heard thumping outside. Mickey, his face red and sweating, his tie askew, dropped the trunk he was dragging, and then, with a grunt, let the one on his shoulder slide to the ground. He straightened up, wiped his face with his sleeve and stepped inside. Kenny moved over to make room for him. He watched as Mickey looked around the shack, his eyes sweeping from the bedroom on the right, across the central room, to Sally curled up on the bed on the left. Kenny saw him take in the woodstove, the kerosene lamp, the single hard bed.

A look came over Mickey's face—or, rather, a series of looks. Confusion. Shock. Rage.

"Mickey," Mom began, reaching for him, but he threw off her hand.

"No!" he bellowed. "I won't! They can't do this!"

He stamped his foot. The floorboards shook.

"Mickey," Kenny said, alarmed, but Mickey ignored him.

He pounded his fist against the door frame. "It's over! It's all over!"

"Mickey, please!" Mom cried. "Stop! You mustn't."

Mickey's knuckles started bleeding. He kept pounding. "No! No!"

Kenny flinched at each blow. Sally jerked awake and started crying.

Kenny glanced at Tak and his mother. They were both staring at Mickey in horror.

Mickey ran outside and picked up a length of wood that was lying on the ground. Rushing inside, he began to bash it against the door frame. "I can't! I won't!" Splinters of wood flew about.

"Mitsuo! Please stop!" Mom begged, holding Sally, who was cowering against her.

Mickey kept pounding. "It's no good! It's over!" The piece of wood disintegrated with every thud.

People came running from nearby cabins.

"Who is it?"

"What a commotion!"

Mom covered her face with her hands.

The crowd parted and a voice bellowed, "What is going on here?"

Mr. Richardson strode into the cabin. He reached for Mickey's arm, but Mickey shook him off.

"No! It's not fair! I won't!"

"Stop this at once!"

Mickey flung away the small club that remained and went back to banging his fist on the wall, shouting incoherently. Mr. Richardson reached for him again, and this time he managed to hold on. Mickey flailed, but he couldn't get free. Then, as if suddenly realizing where he was and what he was doing, he stopped struggling. He slumped, almost falling, his sports jacket half off. Mr. Richardson jerked him up. Mickey panted, cradling his right hand in his left. His hair fell in his face and sweat poured down him. All of them—Kenny, Mickey, Sally, Mom and Mr. Richardson—crowded in the small space inside the doorway. Tak and his mother cowered in the side bedroom.

"What is the meaning of this?" Mr. Richardson shouted, giving Mickey a shake.

Mickey gasped, pulling his hand into his chest.

"Oh, sir, I am so sorry," Mom began.

There was a commotion at the door, and the RCMP officer, Constable Murphy, stepped in. "Harley, what's going on?"

"This ruffian has been causing a disturbance, that's what," Mr. Richardson answered. "Destroying government property. Engaging in riotous behavior. This is illegal. Subversive. You've got to arrest him, Daniel."

No! Kenny thought. *They wouldn't. They couldn't.*

"Please, no!" Mom cried, addressing the policeman. "He didn't mean it, sir. He didn't know what he was doing—"

Mr. Richardson shook his head. "That's the law, ma'am. I won't have any breaches of security in my camp."

Constable Murphy ran his fingers over the gouge in the doorframe. "This *is* serious."

"You bet it is," Mr. Richardson said. "I want you to charge this troublemaker and send him to the prisoner-of-war camp in Ontario."

Kenny gaped. *Send Mickey away? To the prisoner-of-war camp? Where Mr. Watanabe is?* He glanced at his brother, expecting to see shock. Fear. But Mickey only looked blank, empty, like a party balloon that has lost its air.

"No!" Mom wailed. She held out her hands toward the two men. "Please! He's my eldest. My husband is in the camp at Revelstoke. He's a good boy, really. An Asahi! He's not himself. The shock—"

A murmur of voices was heard outside, and then Nakata-sensei came through the crowd. Kenny felt a breath of hope. Nakata-sensei would help.

"Oh, Sensei!" Mom said, seizing his hands. "Thank God you're here. Please . . . tell them . . . don't let them send Mickey away."

"Send him away?" Nakata-sensei asked. "Whatever for?"

Mr. Richardson angrily ran through what Mickey had done and repeated that insurgents were to be sent to the prisoner-of-war camp in Angler, Ontario.

Nakata-sensei bowed to Mr. Richardson. "Sir, I know this young man, and I can assure you that he is no insurgent. He is an upstanding boy."

"He destroyed government property!"

"Yes, he did," Nakata-sensei agreed, "and he should make restitution. But I humbly ask you not to send him away. This poor mother depends on him, with her two young children."

"He should have thought of that before he started acting in a violent manner."

Nakata-sensei looked gravely at Mickey. He took a step closer and touched Mickey's right hand. Mickey jerked back.

"Mickey! You're injured."

"Serves him right," Mr. Richardson muttered.

Constable Murphy carefully examined Mickey's hand. Mickey gasped, and sweat rolled down his face, but he didn't cry out.

"It appears to be broken," Constable Murphy said.

"That makes no difference—" Mr. Richardson began.

"Harley, he's got to have it treated," Constable Murphy said in a low voice. "He should go to hospital—"

"He must be punished!"

"Sir, if I may," Nakata-sensei said. "You are correct. He has done wrong. But surely he should have his injury tended to first. Let him be treated. Then you will determine what his punishment should be. Perhaps he could make amends by performing work in town, or here in the camp."

Constable Murphy brightened. "That's an excellent idea. After all, he *is* young, as the reverend says—"

Mr. Richardson turned to him. "You're not seriously thinking of letting him off!"

"No. This isn't letting him off. He'll have to make restitution. But I think we can show compassion in this case, Harley. If he doesn't cooperate, that's another story. Then we'll have to bring up charges."

"Please, sir," Mom whispered to the officer.

"There had better not be any more disturbances!" Mr. Richardson thundered.

"There won't be. I promise you, sir," Nakata-sensei said.

Mr. Richardson scowled. "Very well. He may be admitted to hospital. For now."

"Thank you, sir," Mom said, bowing first to Constable Murphy and then to Mr. Richardson.

Mr. Richardson left. Constable Murphy took Mickey by his good arm. Just before he stepped through the doorway, Mickey looked back. He didn't say anything, but Kenny could see the shame in his eyes.

As Mickey and Constable Murphy made their way through the crowd, Kenny heard the murmurs.

"Such dishonor."

"Who is it?"

"An Asahi, no less."

People dispersed and went back to their cabins.

Kenny looked at Mom. She had sunk to her knees and buried her face in her hands. Sally clung to her, sucking her thumb.

What happened? Kenny thought. This wasn't Mickey. This wasn't the brother he knew, the humble baseball hero. The pride of the family, of the team, of the community. The older brother who was always there, looking out for Kenny, protecting him.

A jolt of terror stabbed Kenny, and he ran outside. But the path that Constable Murphy and Mickey had taken was empty. Mickey was gone.

Kenny started shaking.

What are we going to do without Mickey?

13

Looking at the empty path, Kenny remembered the two suitcases that he and Mickey had left behind. He dragged them back to the shack one at a time, keeping his head down, hoping no one would recognize him. But he couldn't block out the murmurs.

"Isn't that the brother?"

"What a disgrace for the family . . ."

"I heard he was an Asahi . . ."

He forced himself not to turn and look.

There was no room for the suitcases on the floor, so he shoved them under the bed, along with the other suitcases and trunks.

Dinnertime came. Mom didn't even try to light the woodstove. She, Sally and Kenny sat cross-legged on the bed and finished the food from the train. Kenny scraped up the last grain of rice. He was still hungry.

Sally whispered, "I have to *go*."

Kenny looked at Mom. She stared into space, rubbing one thumb over the other. Kenny held out his hand. "Come on, Sal."

Outside, he looked around. A wooden building, slightly smaller than the shack, perched on a rise a short distance away. *That must be the outhouse*, he thought. On one side, men and boys waited for a turn at one of three holes cut into a wooden platform. Kenny and Sally walked around to the other side. Women and girls lined up in front of three tiny stalls, each with a door. Eyes downcast, they looked embarrassed and did not talk.

Kenny stood in line with Sally. When it was her turn, she gave Kenny a piteous look but went inside. She came out, her face red.

"I don't like this place," she said.

Kenny had no answer.

Mom waited until dark to go to the outhouse. Kenny knew she was too ashamed to show her face outside.

The bed was big enough for only two people. Mom and Sally slept in it, Kenny on a blanket on the floor. He tried lying on his back; his shoulder blades poked into the wooden boards. He rolled onto his side. His hip ached. He tried his stomach. His ribs hurt. So it went all night.

Each time he woke up, he heard the muffled sound of Mom crying into her pillow.

In the morning, tired and sore, he went to the sink to wash up. But there was no tap. No running water. The sink emptied water but did not supply it.

Then Kenny noticed metal buckets stacked up next to the woodstove. *We've got to haul water?* he thought. *I can't do that.*

But they had to have water. And with Dad gone and Mickey in the hospital, that left him.

He took two buckets and went outside, trying to figure out where to fill them. Some people were walking back from the direction of the lake, lugging what looked like full buckets.

All that way!

Walking past the shacks, Kenny heard the sleepy voices of people waking up, the cries of hungry babies. He turned a corner. Four more shacks were under construction. The sound of hammers made a stuttering staccato, joined by the rasp of saws. Even though it was early morning, workers were already hauling lumber and climbing ladders. They seemed to move in double-time, as if they were in a race with the season.

Past the construction zone, a few dozen canvas tents stood on a patch of trampled-down meadow. People were crawling out onto the damp grass, stretching stiffly, or boiling water for tea on open-air gas burners.

Those poor people, Kenny thought. Watching them, he felt guilty that he and Mom and Sally were lucky enough to have been given a shack.

Then he thought: *Lucky?*

At the edge of the camp, the land sloped down toward the lakeshore. As Kenny started down, he saw a boy about his age coming up, laden with two full buckets.

"Excuse me," Kenny said, pointing toward the lake, "is that where we get water?"

"Only for washing," the boy said. "For drinking water, you have to go to the creek, downstream from the bridge."

Kenny groaned. One trip to the lake and another to the creek. *How am I going to do that with my weak arms?*

The trail plunged downhill, and Kenny slithered the rest of the way down to the water. When he got there, he saw that a dozen or so people were standing on a gravelly beach, dipping their buckets into the lake. It was hard, Kenny saw, to fill up your bucket without wading in so deep that your shoes got wet. Then he saw that there was a large flat boulder overhanging the water, and a boy was squatting on it, leaning over to dip his bucket in. That looked like a better idea, so Kenny decided to wait until the boy was finished and then climb out onto the rock.

After a moment, the boy stood up. He was tall and skinny. When the boy lifted his buckets and turned, Kenny recognized him.

"Dai!" he called, and his friend looked up and grinned. As Dai gingerly made his way across the top of the boulder, his glasses slipped down his nose. Reaching with one long leg and then another, he stepped off the rock and put his two buckets down beside Kenny.

"Whew," he said, pushing his glasses back up. "That was tricky. But it beats getting your feet wet. See, I calculated that if I lowered the bucket at a sixty-degree angle, it would fill up—"

Kenny put up his hand. "Dai, spare me."

Dai chuckled. "Sorry. Say, want me to wait for you?"

"Sure."

Kenny stepped onto a lower rock and pushed off from

there onto the boulder. Puddles of water sat in depressions on its surface—clearly other people had spilled water here—and his foot slipped. He tottered briefly, then righted himself. He knelt down and lowered one bucket into the water. When he lifted it back up, some water slopped out, soaking his trousers. Ooh, it was cold. Goose bumps shivered up his body.

Once the second bucket was full, Kenny stood and lifted them both. Lord, they were heavy. He baby-stepped across the boulder. So far, so good. Then, as he felt with his foot for the lower rock, he missed and went down hard on his knee. *Ow!* One bucket fell and emptied. Kenny's knee smarted, and when he stood up he saw that he had ripped his pants. Blood was oozing through the hole.

He heard a guffaw. He turned. Tak. Tak standing on the beach, holding two buckets, watching.

Of course Tak has to be right there at this moment, Kenny thought.

"You okay, Kenny?" Dai called.

His face burning, Kenny nodded. He retrieved the fallen bucket and refilled it. Somehow he made it off the boulder safely.

Kenny and Dai started back up the hill with their buckets. At first it wasn't so bad; there was a pleasant stretching in Kenny's shoulders, and it was good to feel his arm muscles working. He and Dai chatted about the shacks, about how their poor mothers were ever going to figure out how to cook on a woodstove, about annoying little sisters.

Soon, though, Kenny couldn't talk anymore. His arms began to ache. His breath came harder. Dai, too, fell silent. The buckets banged against Kenny's legs, bruising him and soaking his already-wet trousers. He wanted to stop and rest, and he sensed that Dai did, too, but neither wanted to be the first to stop.

His arms were screaming. His heart started pounding.

He couldn't help it. He put his buckets down and stood, panting. Immediately, Dai did the same, shooting Kenny a grateful look.

Just then Tak strode along. His face was red and there were beads of sweat on his forehead, but he didn't stop. "Having trouble, boys?" he said, walking past them. "Too bad about your trousers, Kenny."

Kenny gritted his teeth.

"Don't listen, Kenny," Dai said in a low voice.

But of course he did. Even the sight of Tak up ahead, stopping and setting his buckets down for a moment, shaking out his arms, and glancing over his shoulder to see if they had seen, didn't cheer him up. He had tripped and made a fool of himself, and Mom was going to be upset about his trousers, and Mickey was gone, and he, Kenny, was going to have to haul water, and that meant that he was going to have to put up with Tak's smirk every single day because the truth was that Tak was strong, and he, Kenny, was a weakling.

He lifted the buckets and staggered the rest of the way to the cabin.

14

There were a thousand complaints.

There was no room in the shack. Whenever Mom slid the trunks and suitcases out from under the bed to search for clothes, she scattered Sally's "dolls"—rocks with faces drawn on them—which she had lined up on the floor.

Watching the rocks roll in different directions, Sally burst into tears. "I hate it here! I want to go home! When can we go home, Mommy?"

Mom shrugged. "I don't know, Sally. Try to make the best of it."

Sally threw herself on the bed.

She wasn't the only one who felt cramped. Kenny collided with Tak when they were coming in or going out for water. Mom and Mrs. Watanabe got in each other's way when they were both using the sink and reaching for wash water from the bucket.

Nor was there any place to put their things. When they had first arrived, Mom had taken out all the clothing, hers and Sally's and Mickey's and Kenny's, and laid everything out in piles on the bed. She had taken out the picture of the family, which she had brought from the living room mantel. But when she looked around and saw that there were no shelves, no hooks, no dressers—and no room for a dresser even if there had been one—she groaned and threw everything back into the suitcases.

There wasn't enough light. Even though it was now June and the days were long, when it finally did get dark, the two kerosene lamps created only a small, dim, yellowish dome of light. If someone took one of them to the outhouse, half the shack was plunged into darkness. Even when both were lit, it wasn't bright enough to read, or sew, or write.

Kenny's back ached from sleeping on the floor. Blisters formed on his hands from carrying the buckets. They rubbed and hurt. Every time he went to fetch water, he had to put the buckets down and blow on his hands, trying to cool them. The blisters popped and clear fluid leaked out, and then they formed and popped again, until finally the skin rubbed raw and hurt even more.

Worst of all, though, was the problem of food. Or, rather, cooking. Once the food from the train was gone, Mom scrounged around in one of the trunks and came up with some rice crackers. After that she softened some nori in cold water and served it with raw tofu. She made a wide berth around the woodstove.

After a few days, Kenny's stomach was growling.

"Mommy, I'm hungry," Sally whined.

"Me, too," Kenny said.

A flush spread up Mom's face. She rooted around in the trunk and found the sack of rice and the rice pot. She filled the pot with water from the bucket.

The shacks had been stocked with a supply of firewood: small logs, thicker chunks of wood, thin strips of wood and a box of matches. Mom stopped three steps from the cookstove, staring at it as if it were a dangerous animal. She rubbed her thumbs together. "What . . . how . . . ?"

"I guess you start with the skinny pieces and then add the fat ones," Kenny said.

He opened the small door on the left side of the stove and placed several of the thin pieces inside. Mom lit a match and held it to one of the wisps. It flamed briefly, then went out.

She lit another match. The match went out before the wood could catch.

The third match lit. One skinny piece of wood caught and crackled. Then another.

"Quick!" Mom said, and Kenny pushed a thicker piece on top of the skinny ones. Flames licked along its bottom. Then they collapsed and turned to smoke, which poured out of the stove.

Kenny waved his hand to clear it away. When that didn't work, he jammed the firebox door shut. Smoke continued to leak out.

"I'm hungry! I want rice!" Sally wailed.

Coughing, Mom ran out of the cabin. Kenny followed, his eyes streaming. Mom sat down on the doorstep and put her hands over her face.

If only Dad was here, Kenny thought. He stared at Mom, sitting there with her shoulders slumped.

He ran for Nakata-sensei.

The problem, it turned out, was something called a flue, an iron disk in the stovepipe that you turned to control the fire—open, if you wanted the fire to burn briskly, and closed, if you wanted to bank it down.

With Nakata-sensei's help, Mom got a fire going. It took a long time to get it to burn hot, and even longer for the water to boil. And then the water boiled down, and the rice came out half-cooked and hard. Mom served it into bowls, and they made a table by propping a slab of wood over two cut-off ends from wooden boards. The "table" was a foot high. They sat cross-legged on the floor.

Sally stirred the hard bits with her chopsticks. "I want my old food. I'm not eating this." Mom did something Kenny had never seen her do. She shrugged. "Then don't."

Sally, clearly expecting Mom to cook her something else, or at least sympathize with her, turned wounded eyes on Mom. She lifted a bite with her chopsticks and chewed, crunching loudly.

Mom shot Kenny a smile. It was the first one she'd given since they'd arrived in the camp.

If Mom was bad, Mrs. Watanabe was worse. She sat on her bed and wrung her hands.

"I can't . . ."

"I need Min . . ."

"This is an outrage . . ."

"I simply can't live like this . . ."

She stayed in her fancy traveling clothes, which became more and more bedraggled, and made no attempt to cook. One day when the two boys were alone in the shack, Kenny saw Tak go through their basket from the train, emptying a container of dumplings and a jar of *tsukemono*. When those were gone, Tak rooted around in their trunk. He came up empty.

He glared. "What are you looking at, Sakamoto?"

"Nothing."

Tak stomped out.

After several days, Mom was getting the hang of the cookstove. It could still reduce her to tears when it burned too hot or too cold, when it smoked, when the food came out scorched or raw, when, distracted by other tasks, she forgot to tend the fire and it went out. But she could make oatmeal and tea and stir-fried tofu, and Kenny and Sally didn't starve.

One evening, when Tak was sitting on the edge of his bed, watching while the Sakamotos ate, Mom said, "Here, Tak, have some soup."

Tak blushed. "No, thank you, Mrs. Sakamoto."

"Really, there's plenty."

Tak looked at his mother, who waved a hand. "Go ahead, dear. I just don't feel up to it."

With a bow, Tak accepted a bowl of soup from Mom and joined them at the table on the floor. He ate with his eyes downcast, then returned the bowl with a bow.

"Thank you, Mrs. Sakamoto."

"That's all right. I can't bear to see a boy go hungry."

Tak flushed a deep red.

Kenny turned away. *If it were me, I wouldn't want anyone to pity me either.*

Mrs. Watanabe must have heard Mom, because the next night, after Mom finished at the cookstove, she came into the kitchen with ingredients and utensils. Mom nodded at her. "Would you like me to show you how, Mrs. Watanabe?"

"No, thank you," Mrs. Watanabe returned curtly.

"Very well," Mom said. "Come, Kenny and Sally, let's visit Nakata-sensei."

Once outside, Sally said in a stage whisper, "Why did we have to leave, Mommy?"

"Oh, I thought they could use some privacy," Mom said.

An hour later, when they returned, the kitchen was

empty. Scorched rice was stuck to the woodstove, dirty dishes were sitting on the makeshift table, and a pan with stuck-on tofu was smoking on the stove.

Sounds of sniffling came from the other room.

Mom put her hands on her hips. "Mrs. Watanabe, you cannot leave the kitchen like this!"

A loud sniffle. "I failed . . . I can't cope . . ."

"That's no excuse!"

There was a gasp, and Mrs. Watanabe, tears rolling down her cheeks, came into the kitchen. Her dress was splotched with something wet, and her hair, usually coiffed neatly in a permanent wave, was in disarray. Tak followed, looking embarrassed.

"How can you speak to me like that? I'm not used to living in such conditions, my husband is far away, who knows when—or if—I will ever see him again—"

"We're all without our husbands, Mrs. Watanabe," Mom said. "We all have hardships. But here we are. We have to share this kitchen, and you simply can't make a mess and not clean it up."

Kenny gaped. Only days ago, Mom had been lying on her bed, weeping. Now here she was, her chin thrust out, her eyes sparking.

"But . . . it's so easy for you . . . you know how . . . you don't fall apart . . ."

"What?" Mom said. "That's practically all I've done since we got here."

Mrs. Watanabe ignored that. "I . . . just . . . can't!" To Kenny's amazement, she threw herself into Mom's arms and started sobbing on her shoulder.

Mom looked startled, but she patted Mrs. Watanabe on the back. "There, there . . . it's all right . . . hush now . . ."

Kenny darted a look at Tak. He was staring at the floor, his face red.

Finally Mrs. Watanabe stopped crying.

"Now," Mom said, taking her hands, "I assure you that I haven't the faintest idea what to do in this horrible place, and I'm just as unhappy to be here as you are. But *shikata ga nai*—it can't be helped. So we have to pull together and do our best. Right, Mrs. Watanabe?"

Tak's mother heaved a sigh. "Please, call me Fumiko."

"Keiko."

The two women nodded at one another. Then they rolled up their sleeves and started cleaning up.

15

After that, things got a little better. Sally still had tantrums when Mom interrupted her play to retrieve things from under the bed. But Mom gave her a couple of old socks, which Sally stuffed with grass to make dolls. Mom sewed on faces, and Sally slept with "Miranda" and "Arabella."

"And at least they don't clunk on the floor, like rocks," Sally said.

Together, Mom and Mrs. Watanabe figured out how to work the cookstove without smoking out the cabin. There were still burned fingers and boiled-over pots, but not as many tears. Usually Mom, who was better at starting the fire, cooked first and left the stove for Mrs. Watanabe, who slowly learned to make a decent meal on it.

Nakata-sensei organized a group of older boys and elderly men to build kitchen tables in each of the shacks.

They attached a slab of wood to the sidewall and propped it up on two legs. They also built a rough bench. That meant that the Sakamotos and Watanabes no longer had to eat on the raised plank on the floor.

Kenny scrounged a bunch of nails and managed to bang them into the wall, smashing his thumb only twice, so Mom was able to hang up some of their clothes. But most of their things—underwear and socks, T-shirts and sweaters, blouses and pajamas—couldn't be hung up, so Kenny and Mom still had to haul suitcases out from under the bed every time they needed those. Kenny promised that he'd find a board and build a shelf, although he had no idea how.

He pounded another nail into the wall over the bed, and Mom put up the family photograph. He and Mom knelt side by side on the bed and looked at it. She ran her finger first over Dad's face, then over Mickey's. Her eyes filled with tears. Kenny's throat felt thick. He turned away. But he was glad the picture was there, all the same.

His blisters hardened into calluses. He and Dai worked out a system where Dai, who had longer arms, went out on the boulder and filled the buckets, and then passed them to Kenny, who waited on shore.

One day when Kenny came back, sweating, and set the buckets down, Mom wiped his forehead. "Oh, Kenny, I worry about you, doing that. It's too much for your heart."

"There's no one else," he said. Then, seeing the look on her face, added, "It's okay, Mom. I'm getting better at it. I can do it."

It's true, he realized. On the way back up the hill, he found that he tired less easily. His arms still ached and his heart still pounded and his breath still came short, but he didn't have to stop and rest as often. Sometimes he secretly felt his arms for muscles. He thought he detected a slight bump.

One day a letter from Susana arrived.

June 20, 1942
Dear Kenny,

Tak Watanabe is in your shack??? Poor you! Is he just as show-offy as ever? All I can say is, ignore Tak. He only THINKS he's great. We both know who's really great.

(You, you idiot.)

Kenny smiled. He could just hear her saying that. She'd poke him with her elbow so he wouldn't get too puffed up about it.

> I miss you. I miss everyone. There's hardly anybody left in our class. Emiko went to a town called Kaslo. Naomi went to an abandoned mining camp in Greenwood. Most of the stores on Powell Street are closed. It's spooky.

Kenny tried to imagine Powell Street empty and abandoned. He couldn't. It was too busy, too lively. Where were the honks of the cars, the rumble of the buses, the smells of fish and tea, the familiar faces of the shopkeepers?

> I keep asking Mama and Papa when you are coming back. They say they don't know. They go to meetings and write letters. So far nobody is listening. But they'll keep trying. You can count on that.

Good old Auntie Miriam and Uncle Jake, Kenny thought. Tears stung his eyes.

I didn't mean for this letter to be so sad. Here's something to cheer you up. Yesterday Keith McAlary swiped some little kid's lunch box. It opened and a banana fell out and Keith stepped on it and banana mushed all over his shoe. He was hopping around, trying to shake it off. Serves him right!

Your friend,
Susana

Kenny laughed, picturing Keith madly shaking his foot. Boy, it felt good to laugh. He couldn't remember the last time he had done it.

Ignore Tak, Susana had written. That was easier said than done. Tak had a way of being exactly where Kenny didn't want him to be.

When Mom was out in the camp doing things, Kenny had to watch Sally. And not just watch her. Get down on the floor and play with "Miranda" and "Arabella," the sock dolls.

One day, when Kenny was minding Sally, she held up Miranda and poked Kenny's sock with it. "Come on, Arabella, let's dance." Kenny was half-heartedly swooping his sock back and forth, cheek to cheek with Sally's, humming a tune, when Tak came in.

He hooted. "Dolls! Oh, dance with me, darling!"

Kenny scowled, blushing.

Most of the time, though, Tak was nowhere to be found. Kenny saw him roaming around the camp and suspected that he was looking for someone, anyone, other than Kenny and Dai to chum around with. Sure enough, after a few days, Tak started hanging around with two new boys. One had a round, friendly face and sticking-out ears. Solidly built, he looked to Kenny as if he'd be a strong hitter. The other was small and wiry; he'd probably be a good base runner. They looked like nice fellows. But they were Tak's now. They followed him around, skipping rocks when he skipped rocks, blowing into blades of grass when he did. They ran races, and even though Kenny could tell that the short boy could have beaten Tak, the boy held back.

"I win," Tak said.

"You're fast," the strong-looking boy said.

"Well, I was one of the best base runners on the Clovers last year."

"You were? Wow!"

"Yeah, and I would have made it again, only . . ."

Do not *feel sorry for him*, Kenny told himself.

———

Another letter arrived from Dad. He was still at the road camp in Revelstoke.

> The work is hard. Every day we dig up tree roots, cut
> logs and rake gravel. The men say ███████████████
> ███████████ But at least we have decent rice and
> some meat. Not many vegetables, though. How I long
> for your cooking, Keiko! I miss you all terribly. At least
> I can rest, knowing that Mickey is taking care of you.

Kenny stared at Mom. "You didn't tell him?" He knew she had written a letter to Dad, addressed to the Revelstoke road camp.

She bowed her head. "I couldn't. I hated to lie, Kenny, but . . . it would worry him so, to think of us left all on our own. And the shame . . ." She put her hands over her face.

Kenny patted Mom's shoulder, but she only gave a muffled sob. She had so far managed to hold her head up around the camp, but Kenny had heard her at night, crying into her pillow after Sally was asleep.

Kenny sought out Nakata-sensei. The minister led him to Mr. Richardson's office. "Sir," Nakata-sensei said, "would you allow Mrs. Sakamoto to visit her son in hospital? It would ease her heart."

"That would be highly irregular," Mr. Richardson blustered, "and I see no reason to mollycoddle a known miscreant." But in the end he gave permission for Mom, Kenny and Nakata-sensei to go into New Denver.

Kenny ran back to the shack with the news. Mom brightened immediately. She washed her face and put on a clean dress. She filled a basket with some of Mickey's favorite foods. Mrs. Watanabe offered to watch Sally, who was deemed too young to go.

Kenny and Mom met Nakata-sensei at the entrance to the camp. When Nakata-sensei set off down the road, Kenny looked around. "Aren't we going to have a guard or anything?"

Nakata-sensei turned back with a smile. "No need, my boy. Where would we escape to?"

He gestured with his arm, and as Kenny looked around at the rugged mountains, the wild forests and the vast lake that surrounded them, he realized that Nakata-sensei was right. There was no need for a guard. No need for a fence around the camp. The wilderness was more confining than any bars.

———

After walking three miles along the highway, they turned down a street called 6th Avenue and headed toward the lake. In the distance, Kenny heard the sound of children playing. *Recess*, he realized. School was still in session. He'd forgotten all about school. To his surprise, he missed it.

They walked on. There weren't many people about, and those that were stared at them as if they were martians. A man mowing his lawn even spat in their direction. But then a young woman walking with two toddlers, one on each hand, smiled.

As they passed a grocery store, two women came out carrying bags. Nakata-sensei made a small bow. "Good afternoon, ladies."

The women turned to each other. Kenny heard one whisper to the other, "They speak English!"

He rolled his eyes. *How ignorant can you get? Of course we speak English. We're Canadian!*

They turned right on Kildare Street and came to a large house with a sign over the doorway that said SLOCAN COMMUNITY HOSPITAL. Kenny stopped short.

Will Mickey be better?

Will he want to see us?

What if he isn't allowed to come back?

Inside, the minister explained to a woman at the front desk who they were and why they were there. After a delay, during which the woman inspected their basket as if it might contain explosives, a nurse came out front. She introduced herself as Nurse Gregory. She was young, and wore a stiff white cap over soft blond waves. An upside-down watch was pinned to her uniform. She looked curiously at them. *But at least she doesn't seem to hate us, like some of the people on the street*, Kenny thought.

They followed her down a hallway. Kenny caught glimpses of people in beds, the occasional visitor sitting in a chair. An orderly walked by, pushing a trolley of food trays.

Nurse Gregory paused outside a room. "I'm sorry to say, Mrs. Sakamoto, Reverend, that Mr. Sakamoto has not been doing well," she said.

Kenny heard Mom's sharp intake of breath. "Is he sick?"

Nurse Gregory shook her head. "No, not exactly. It's that . . . he doesn't seem to *want* to get well. He's barely eating. When Constable Murphy comes in, he won't talk to him, won't answer questions."

That was the first Kenny had heard that Constable Murphy had visited Mickey. He remembered what the police officer had said: *If he doesn't cooperate, we'll have to bring up charges.* He tensed.

Nurse Gregory pushed open the door. "Mr. Sakamoto," she said in a bright voice, "you have visitors."

Mickey was curled up on top of the bedcovers, facing the wall. A night table held a glass of water. Over the bed, a wooden shelf was attached to the wall with a Bible on it. Drawn curtains kept the room dim.

"Mitsuo!" Mom cried.

Mickey jerked his head up, looked over his shoulder and turned back to the wall. A cast covered his right hand, and he moved his arm awkwardly.

"My son," Nakata-sensei said, touching Mickey's shoulder.

Mickey curled into a tighter ball. "Please go away."

Mom sat on the edge of the bed. She leaned over and kissed Mickey's cheek. He seemed to cringe on the mattress. "Mom, please. I have brought dishonor to you. Leave me."

"No, Mickey. You didn't know what you were doing. You weren't yourself—"

"I shamed you."

"Mickey, your family needs you," Nakata-sensei said.

"I am worthless. Useless."

This was worse than Kenny had expected. He'd expected Mickey to be embarrassed. He'd expected him to be climbing the walls with nervous energy. He'd expected him to be in a bad mood.

But I didn't expect him to just give up.

Kenny thought of the championship game last fall, when the Asahis had been down with two out in the bottom of the ninth. Had Mickey given up then? No! He'd dug deep and come up with the big hit. Where was that spirit now?

Mom opened the basket, taking out containers. "Mickey, you must eat. Look, I brought your favorites. *Mochi*, with salted plums. See? Please, my boy, eat, you'll make yourself sick."

"Good," Mickey said under his breath.

"No! Don't say that!" Mom cried.

"You mustn't talk that way," Nakata-sensei said. "Once your hand is healed, you must apologize to the officials, find a way to pay for the damage and come home."

"Home." Mickey's voice cracked.

"It's not so bad, Mickey," Kenny said. "We have a table and bench now. I've got a system worked out for hauling water—"

Mickey made a strangled noise. "I'm sorry, Kenny. I've let you down. You and everyone."

"It's all right, Mickey. Only come back to us," Mom said.

"I don't want to go on," Mickey said in a low voice.

Kenny started. Mom didn't seem to have heard.

What does Mickey mean by that? That he wants to die? No, he can't. Maybe only that he doesn't want to go back to the camp. Yes, that must be it.

But a chill shivered up Kenny's back just the same.

Back on the street, Mom clutched Nakata-sensei's hand. "Oh, Sensei, what will I do?"

"He'll come around, Mrs. Sakamoto," Nakata-sensei said. But his face was grave.

They walked back in silence. On the way, they passed a large building with a sign that said PROVINCIAL GOVERN-MENT BUILDING. Next to it there was a grassy field, and Kenny spotted a baseball backstop on it, and bases, and two wooden benches on either side of home plate. A couple of RCMP officers, their neckties loosened and their shirtsleeves rolled up, were tossing a baseball back and forth.

A baseball field! Kenny realized. *Those lucky ducks. There's sure nothing like it at the camp.*

He thought of Mickey in his Asahi uniform, clouting the winning run. *If those cops had seen Mickey then, they'd know what a baseball player really is.*

Then he thought of Mickey pounding his fist on the wall of the shack, shouting, "It's over! It's all over!" Of Mickey in his hospital room, curled up on his bed.

I've got to do something, Kenny thought. *Something to snap Mickey out of it.*

But what?

On the way back to the camp, Kenny, Mom and Nakata-sensei stopped at the grocery store. Mom had brought some money from home, and part of Dad's wages went to the camp to pay for the family's expenses.

The man behind the counter gawked when they walked in. Two women moved away, and a man holding a little boy by the hand left, saying over his shoulder, "I'll come back later."

Kenny's face burned.

While the grocer waited on first one of the women and then the other, more customers arrived. After the second woman had paid and left, Mom stepped forward, ready to place her order.

The grocer turned to a young mother who had come in with a baby carriage. "Good afternoon, Mrs. Cookson, what can I do for you?"

Kenny exchanged a look with Mom. She pressed her lips together.

Maybe he took the lady first because she has a baby, Kenny thought.

But after she was finished, the man served another woman, and then a man who had just walked in. Finally all the other customers were gone. The grocer turned to Mom, frowning. "Yes?"

"Yes, sir, may I have three tofu cakes and a bottle of shoyu please?"

"What? Speak English."

Mom's cheeks turned crimson. Nakata-sensei stepped forward. "Perhaps you didn't understand, sir. Mrs. Sakamoto here would like to buy some bean curd cakes and soya sauce."

"We don't have any Jap foods," the grocer snapped.

Kenny, Mom and Nakata-sensei stood there. Then they turned and left.

16

"Any news of the war?"

Often, Kenny heard people ask this of one another. The answer was always a shake of the head. Japanese Canadians were not allowed to have radios or newspapers, and no one knew what was happening in the world outside the borders of the camp.

One day in early July, when Mrs. Kimura, Dai's mother, was in the camp supervisor's office, she spotted an open newspaper on Mr. Richardson's desk. JAPAN TAKES GUADALCANAL, the headline read.

The news spread through the camp, whispered from one person to another.

A group gathered near the outhouses. "What does it mean, Sensei?" Mom asked Nakata-sensei. "Is Japan winning the war?"

The minister looked grim. "I don't know, Mrs. Sakamoto. It doesn't sound good."

Kenny wondered how Mom felt about the news. If Japan won, her parents might be safe. *But what would that mean for us?* he wondered.

"Surely the Allies will take the island back," an older man said.

"Let's hope so," Nakata-sensei said. "Remember that this is only one battle. It's not over yet."

"All I know is, there's no end in sight to the war," Mrs. Kimura said.

"Or to this internment," her father-in-law said.

Sighing, people dispersed back to their shacks.

Another letter arrived from Susana. Kenny tore it open.

July 6, 1942
Dear Kenny,

I am so bored. Do you want to know how bored I am? The other day I played with Maggie Resnick, and all she wanted to do was look at the clothes in the Eaton's catalog. Frills and ribbons and lace. Ugh. She's not even interested in baseball.

Kenny laughed out loud, picturing Susana fidgeting and rolling her eyes while Maggie oohed and aahed over the dresses in the catalog.

Speaking of baseball, things are really dead without the Asahis. Papa and I have been following the Vancouver Capilanos. They have a left-handed pitcher named Glenn Elliott who's pretty good, but, honestly, they're not as exciting to watch as the Asahis. Their bunting is pathetic!

How is your family? Have you heard from Uncle Harry? How is Auntie Keiko holding up? Has Mickey got all the kids in the camp playing ball? Is Sally throwing fits? (Even if she is, she couldn't be as bad as Gittie. Believe me.) And how about you?

Your friend,
Susana

P.S. A government person came around and wanted to look in your house, but Mama chased him away. She

said to tell Auntie Keiko that everything is okay and
that all your things are safe you-know-where.

Kenny held the paper in both hands, missing her.

Has Mickey got all the kids in the camp playing ball? He
hadn't told her about Mickey. He'd wanted to, but somehow he'd felt that if Dad didn't know, it wasn't right for
Kenny to tell her. But how he wished he could. *What
should we do, Susana?* he'd say, and even if she didn't have
any answers, it would make him feel better knowing that
she was concerned, too.

Is Sally throwing fits? Amazingly, the answer was no!
Not anymore. It had changed on the day he and Mom and
Nakata-sensei had gone into town to see Mickey. They
had come home to find Sally and Mrs. Watanabe dressed
in kimonos, dancing in the narrow space between the
front door and the woodstove.

"Guess what, Mom!" Sally yelled, running to greet her.
"Mrs. Watanabe is teaching me."

Mrs. Watanabe bowed. "I hope you don't mind, Keiko.
I took the liberty. When I found out that Sally was studying *odori*—"

"She says I'm really talented, Mom!"

"Sally!" Mom scolded, but she smiled.

"Yes, indeed, Keiko, she has true feeling," Mrs. Watanabe said.

After that, Sally and Mrs. Watanabe spent at least an hour together every day. That was one hour when Kenny didn't have to watch Sally.

And Sally had stopped sucking her thumb, too!

Kenny smoothed out Susana's letter on the kitchen table and went to fetch paper from his suitcase to write her back. Squatting down, he pulled Mom's trunk out from under the bed, then Sally's suitcase, and finally his own. This was getting really tiresome, and it wasn't just the suitcases. Jars of rice, sugar, beans and spices were stacked in a wooden box near the stove, and every time Mom needed one ingredient, she had to empty the box to find it, then repack everything. There was no place to put books, or Mom's sewing basket, or their clock.

If only we had a shelf, Kenny thought, taking out the paper and shoving his suitcase back under the bed. *But how do you build one?* He remembered the shelf in Mickey's hospital room. It had been attached to the wall, but it had to have been propped up in some way. It didn't have legs, like the table the workers had built, but something held it up. He tried to remember, and in his mind's eye saw a couple of triangular pieces of wood jutting out from the wall, supporting it from beneath.

That might work. If he could find, or make, two wooden triangles and nail them to the wall, then a board could sit on their flat edges. It was worth a try, anyway.

Kenny remembered seeing scraps of wood on a vacant piece of land across the road from the outermost group of shacks, near where Carpenter Creek emptied into the lake. The workers who were building shacks tossed the cut-off ends of boards and odd-shaped pieces of wood there. Sometimes he'd seen people sorting through the scraps, searching for building materials.

I'll go look right now, he thought. Tucking Susana's letter into his pocket, he walked to the vacant field. There were thirty shacks built so far, and the pile of discarded lumber was bigger than he'd thought. An area nearly the size of his old school yard was covered with scrap wood, broken roof shakes and torn pieces of tar paper. Kenny sighed. *How will I find the right-size pieces of wood in this mess?*

He started sorting through the nearest pile, trying to find the shapes of the supports and the board he needed among the odd-shaped scraps. He nudged a promising

piece with his toe, then, discovering it had bent nails pro-
truding from it, flung it away.

Maybe it was Susana's letter, with her talk about baseball. Maybe it was what caught his eye as he watched the
piece of wood land. But Kenny noticed something. The
vacant lot was roughly diamond-shaped. He was standing
at one pointy end. It widened out where the road veered
away from the creek, and then narrowed to another point
where the road curved back again.

Baseball-field-shaped.

Kenny thought of the baseball field he'd seen in town,
next to the provincial government building. He thought of
the two constables playing catch.

If there's baseball in town, why not here at the camp?

Kenny had no idea how, or if, this vacant lot could be
transformed into a field. But if it could, it would give the
kids in camp something to do—other than their chores.

Kenny remembered his own pathetic attempts to learn
to play, when he'd persuaded Mickey to train him.

Maybe I'll be better this time, he thought. Then he
scoffed at himself. *There isn't any* this time. *All there is, is
an odd-shaped field strewn with debris.*

Then Kenny had another thought.

If there's one thing that can bring Mickey back, it's baseball.

Forgetting about the shelf, he ran to the camp supervisor's office. From inside he heard a woman's voice saying, "But, sir, our children have already lost a month of school. They need their education."

The voice was familiar, but Kenny couldn't place it.

Mr. Richardson snapped, "And I keep telling you, ma'am, that the government has not authorized education for enemy aliens."

"But we would gather the books ourselves, sir. And if we could just have the use of one of the shacks for a schoolhouse—"

"The answer is no."

The door opened, and the woman stepped out. It was Mrs. Kimura, Dai's mother. She hurried past Kenny, looking crestfallen.

Kenny gulped. Mr. Richardson was grumpy at the best of times, and this didn't look like a very good time. Kenny tapped lightly on the open door.

"Yes?" A bark.

Kenny put his head around the door. "Excuse me, sir—"

"What do *you* want?"

Kenny stepped the rest of the way inside. Mr. Richardson was leafing through papers in a folder, turning each one over with a slap. His desk was piled high with folders and books, papers and forms, pens and pads.

"Uh . . . I was wondering . . . you know that vacant lot where the workers throw scrap wood, over by the creek?"

"Yes, what of it?"

"Well, I, uh . . . could we clear it off? And then we could use it—" Kenny stopped. *I don't want to tell him about the baseball field. It's a stupid idea anyway, and he'll only laugh* "—to play on," he finished.

"Absolutely not." Mr. Richardson slammed the file folder shut.

"Absolutely not what?" a voice said.

Kenny turned. It was Constable Murphy. He came in, loosening his tie. "Hot as the dickens out there, Harley. Absolutely not what?"

Mr. Richardson gestured with the file folder. "This young-ster wants us to free up land for a children's playground."

"Not a playground, sir, just a place to play—"

"Why, that's a swell idea," Constable Murphy said, taking off his hat. He looked more closely at Kenny. "I've seen you. You're Mickey Sakamoto's brother, aren't you?"

"That troublemaker," Mr. Richardson muttered.

"Yes, sir."

"And you are . . . ?"

"Kenji Sakamoto, sir. Kenny."

"Well, Kenny, I think that's a terrific idea. What's the problem with it, Harley?"

"Not their land to do with what they please."

"No, of course not. But it *is* just sitting idle. And it's an eyesore to boot," Constable Murphy said.

"Hmph."

"Besides, what's the harm in giving the kids a place to play?"

Kenny remembered that Nurse Gregory had said that Constable Murphy had come in to see Mickey. Now, Constable Murphy smiled, and Kenny's heart lifted. *Maybe this crazy idea has a chance.*

"And it would keep us out of trouble," Kenny added.

Mr. Richardson fixed fierce eyes on him. "It would, would it?"

Kenny quailed. But then he caught an encouraging nod from Constable Murphy. "Yes, sir. Keep us busy and all."

"And what'll you do with all those scraps? Tell me that, eh?"

"Uh . . ." He hadn't thought about that. "Pile them up nice and neat, sir. And people could use them for firewood. Or to make shelves and things."

"Hmmm." For a moment Kenny thought Mr. Richardson was softening, but he frowned again. "And have all you Jap kids stick yourselves with nails and get tetanus? No, thank you."

"We'll be careful, sir. And . . . we'll straighten out the nails and give them back to the workers."

Constable Murphy laughed. "He's got it all figured out, Harley."

Mr. Richardson glared at Kenny. "Oh, all right. But don't come running to me for help. And if anyone gets hurt, I don't want to hear about it."

"Yes, sir."

"Go on, then!"

"Yes, sir!"

As Kenny turned to leave, Constable Murphy winked at him. Kenny smiled back.

He started walking home.

I've got my wish. Now how on earth am I going to do it?

17

Kenny stood at the edge of the vacant field. In his mind's eye, he saw it transformed into the Powell Street Grounds, with a carpet of green grass in the outfield, a tall wire backstop and straight-as-an-arrow chalk lines marking the base paths. But when he looked out and saw the mess of wood and trash in front of him, his heart sank.

This is a crazy idea. Why on earth did I think I could turn this scrap heap into a baseball field?

Then he thought of Mickey in his hospital room, murmuring, "I don't want to go on."

Kenny squared his shoulders. He lifted a two-foot-long board and set it down behind where home plate would be. Then he found several short, stubby pieces of wood. It didn't make sense to pile them on top of the flat board, so he started a separate pile for short pieces nearby.

The next board had a couple of nails sticking out of it. Kenny knew that he had to remove the nails. He'd seen Dad pound nails out of scrap wood by banging their points with a hammer. But Kenny didn't have a hammer. He scouted around and found a flat rock. Pounding it against the points, he was able to push the nails far enough that he could wiggle them out of the wood. But now he had bent nails. He'd promised Mr. Richardson that he'd straighten them out, but for that he'd need a hammer. He started a new pile for bent nails, to be dealt with later.

Back to the field. A three-foot board. Four shakes. A one-foot board. A dozen small board ends. Eight more nails.

The sun beat on Kenny's back. His fingernails chipped where he banged them with the rock. Sweat ran down the back of his neck, mingling with the dirt that coated him. His heart started beating hard. He tried to ignore it. *I'm okay*, he told himself.

He didn't feel okay. He felt tired and shaky.

He straightened up to check his progress. He so far had two uneven piles of scrap wood and a small mound of nails. He had cleared about three square feet of ground.

He sighed.

The next board was wedged under a rock. As Kenny grasped it to pull it free, he felt a splinter pierce his finger. *Ouch!* He pulled the splinter out and sucked his finger.

"What the heck are you doing?"

Kenny whirled around.

Tak was standing there, flanked by his two new friends. Kenny had learned their names. Sammy was the bigger boy, and Jun was the small, fast-looking one. They were Tak's shadows, just like his pals back home.

Tak snorted. "Looking for buried treasure?"

Jun and Sammy laughed.

"No," Kenny said, wiping his still-bleeding finger on his pants. "Just . . . cleaning up. I want to try to make a baseball field."

It slipped out before he could stop himself.

Tak hooted. "A baseball field? Are you out of your mind?" He elbowed Jun. "Play ball! Just watch out for the trash."

Jun laughed. "And good luck finding the bases."

"I've only just started," Kenny said. "I know it doesn't look like anything yet—"

"*Yet?*" Tak said. "How about *never?*"

"It will. I can do it."

"Yeah, sure, Sakamoto," Tak said with a smirk. "You and your strong arms are going to turn this mess into the Powell Street Grounds."

Kenny didn't answer. Jun and Sammy looked at his arms with pitying expressions.

"Well, be sure to let us know when opening day is," Tak said. "Come on, boys."

Chuckling, Jun and Sammy followed Tak across the road. As they walked away, Tak started singing, "Take me out to the ball game, take me out to the crowd . . . ," and the other two joined in.

Kenny watched them go, then turned back to survey the wasteland. *Tak's right*, he thought. He'd been working for only an hour and already his back ached and his arms were tired and his finger was bleeding. And he'd made hardly any progress. And even if he was able to clear all the debris, how was he going to turn this patch of land into a baseball diamond? The ground he'd cleared was a bumpy mix of dirt and gravel, sprouting tufts of weeds. He'd have to smooth it out and make bases and build a backstop.

It's hopeless. I should quit now, forget the whole thing. Sure, he'd have to put up with Tak saying "I told you so."

And Constable Murphy would be disappointed. *But it's better than carrying on with this stupid idea.*

Frustrated, he kicked the board that had given him the splinter.

"Kenny, why are you mad at that board?"

Dai.

"I'm not. It's just—nothing."

Dai pointed at the stacked pieces of wood. "Doesn't look like nothing. You collecting building materials?"

"No, I thought I'd make this into a baseball field. But it was dumb—"

"You mean this vacant lot?"

"Yeah, it sort of has the right shape, but—"

"Hey, you're right." Dai took several steps backward and surveyed the field. "It's not exactly a diamond, more of a trapezoid, and the outfield angle is a bit too acute, but it's close enough."

"Yeah, but there's too much junk, and it'll take forever to clear, and the ground's lumpy, and it'll never work," Kenny said glumly.

"Well, yeah, it does look like a ton of work," Dai agreed. "But that doesn't mean it can't be done."

"It's a huge job just sorting the boards."

"That's easy." Dai walked over to the piles. "Everything three feet or less here. Longer boards over there. Small, irregular pieces in a pile. Shakes over here, to be split for kindling. I figure we can stack up a dozen boards—let's see, they're about three-quarters of an inch thick, so that would make a stack, uh, nine inches high. That ought to be stable. Then we'd have to start a new pile."

"But there's all these nails that have to be taken out."

"I have a hammer."

"You do?" In spite of himself, Kenny felt his hope rising again.

"Yeah. My mother won't mind if I take it."

Kenny looked back over the lot. "It's not going to make a very good field."

"Better than nothing."

Kenny looked at his friend. "You sure you want to do this?"

"Look, Kenny, if it's a choice between hauling garbage out of this field or playing house with my sisters, let me at the field."

Kenny laughed.

Dai had an eye for what to do with the scraps. He could size up a piece of wood and decide instantly where it belonged: short boards, longer boards, scraps of tar paper, shakes. He kept the piles straight, and organized them so that he had to take the fewest steps from one to the next. With Kenny carrying the pieces from the field and handing them to Dai, the work went quickly. Within an hour, the cleared space doubled, then tripled, in size.

Neither Kenny nor Dai was good at straightening the bent nails. It was easier to pound and claw them out of the boards with the hammer than with the rock, but flattening them out was another matter. Kenny bashed his thumb. Dai actually made the kinks worse. They decided to put all the nails in a pile for the time being and worry about them later.

The next day, Tak, Sammy and Jun came by again. "Oh, so now you're in on this crazy scheme, Dai?" Tak said.

"Yup."

"*Two* idiots," Tak said, rolling his eyes, and Jun chuckled.

Sammy whistled. "Wow, they've really done a lot."

Tak snorted. "Yeah, in another ten years the ground might be cleared. And it still won't look like a baseball diamond."

"Just moving junk from one place to another," Jun said. "Silly."

"They're nearly halfway to the pitcher's mound," Sammy pointed out.

"What pitcher's mound?" Tak said.

"Wait and see," Kenny said. He and Dai had been at it for over an hour. With a larger space cleared, he had to carry each piece farther, and it was tiring. He'd just been about to suggest that they knock off for the day, but not now. Not with Tak there. He forced himself to pick up another board and carry it over to Dai.

Sammy stepped forward. "Good system you got going."

"Thanks, Sammy."

"Uh, you fellas want some help?"

"Sammy! Don't be a fool," Tak said.

Sammy blushed. "It's something to do. And it'd be fun to play ball again."

"No one'll ever play ball on this wasteland."

"Can't hurt to try." Sammy walked over to Kenny. "What do you want me to do?"

Kenny's mouth fell open. *Someone's asking* me *what to do?* "Well . . . if you hand me pieces, and then I hand them to Dai, that'll make things go faster."

"Like an assembly line, right?"

Kenny grinned. "Right."

"Sure." Sammy moved out to the edge of the cleared space.

"If you want to waste your time, Sammy, that's your business," Tak said. "Come on, Jun."

Jun hesitated, but followed Tak back toward the camp.

Sammy, Kenny and Dai worked in silence for a while. Sammy positioned himself farther out, handing scraps to Kenny, who handed them to Dai to sort. By the time Kenny turned back, Sammy was ready with the next piece. His body settled into a rhythm: step, receive, turn, step, hand over; step, receive, turn, step, hand over.

Sammy handed a board to Kenny. "I hear your brother is an Asahi."

Kenny glanced at him. *Is Sammy about to bring up Mickey's shameful outburst?* "Yeah, he is," he said warily.

"He hit the winning run in the Pacific Northwest League championship last fall," Dai told him.

Sammy looked at Kenny. "He's *that* guy? Wow!"

"Amazing hitter," Dai said. "Batted .335 on the season—as a rookie."

"Holy cow!"

Kenny handed the board to Dai. He didn't even notice the ache in his arms.

———

A couple of days later, while the three boys were working, Kenny heard someone call his name. He looked up, his arms full of boards. Sally. And Mom.

Uh-oh.

Sally skipped over. "We heard what you were doing. We came to see."

Kenny looked past her to Mom. She didn't say anything.

Sally opened big eyes. "Boy, that's sure a lot of wood you got there. What are you going to do with it all?"

Before Kenny could answer, Mom pulled him aside. "Kenny, you shouldn't be doing this. Such hard work."

Kenny squirmed. "It's okay, Mom." Looking over his shoulder, he saw his friends watching. "Not now."

"It's heavy, and in the hot sun—"

"Really, Mom, it's okay. I'm being careful."

Mom released him, but Kenny could tell that she wasn't happy. She walked away, looking worried.

A moment later, Dai said under his breath, "Uh-oh. Look who's here."

Kenny looked up, expecting to see Mom coming back. It wasn't her. It was Mr. Richardson, with Constable Murphy. Kenny stiffened. He stood with a broken shake in his hands, waiting. Dai nudged a pile of boards with his foot, straightening their edges.

"Would you look at this, Harley!" Constable Murphy said. "All this free space. And those piles, so organized."

Mr. Richardson strolled out to the edge of the cleared area. "Hmph. Not bad."

"Not bad!" Constable Murphy repeated. "It's terrific. Good work, boys."

"Thanks," Kenny said.

Mr. Richardson went over to Dai's area and examined the piles. He looked impressed, and Kenny thought he might actually say something positive. Then he frowned. "What's with all these nails? You said you'd straighten them—"

"We will, sir," Kenny said.

"We can't have them lying around, waiting to prick people, cause infections. Unsafe. Unsanitary. Won't do."

"We've got a plan, Mr. Richardson," Dai said. "We're . . . uh . . . going to collect them and then straighten them all at once. More efficient."

Quick thinking, Dai, Kenny thought, suppressing a smile.

Mr. Richardson grunted. "See that you do. And soon."

"Yes, sir," Kenny and Dai said together.

Mr. Richardson walked away. Constable Murphy lingered. He squeezed Kenny's shoulder. "Keep up the good work, son."

Kenny waited until they were out of earshot. "That old grump. Would it kill him to say something nice?"

"Guess so," Dai said. He imitated Mr. Richardson's voice. " 'Fine job—agh—ugh—eek!' " He fell to the ground, pretending to die.

Kenny and Sammy laughed.

"At least he didn't tell us we had to stop," Sammy pointed out.

"I'd like to see him try!" Kenny said angrily. "Come on, boys, let's get a move on. We'll show him!"

They set to with renewed energy.

18

As Nurse Gregory led Kenny and Mom to Mickey's room on their next visit a couple of weeks later, she paused in the hallway. "I'm sorry to tell you, ma'am, that Mr. Sakamoto is no better. Maybe worse," she said.

"Is his hand not healing?" Mom asked.

Nurse Gregory shook her head. "It's not that. In fact, the doctor just took his cast off, and the bone appears to have healed well. It's that he's refusing to do his exercises. You see, when a hand is in a cast, it's immobile, and the muscles get weak. So you must do exercises to bring them back to strength. I've shown Mr. Sakamoto the regimen. But he won't do it. He says there's no point. But he must, or his hand *will* become useless." She gave them a worried look.

I like her, Kenny thought. *She cares.*

"The doctor won't release him until he shows signs of

improvement." Nurse Gregory opened the door. "Perhaps you can talk some sense into him."

Mom sighed as if she doubted it.

Mickey lay on his back, staring at the ceiling. The planes of his cheekbones were sharper, and there was a dusting of stubble on his chin. A rubber ball, a thick elastic band and a small barbell sat on the night table.

Kenny glanced at Mickey's hand. It was pale where the cast had been, and looked a little shrunken, but it wasn't deformed or anything.

Mom gently took his injured hand. "Mickey, the nurse told us about the exercises. You must do them. You must!"

She tried to hand him the rubber ball, but he waved it away. "What's the point?"

"What do you mean? Of course there's a point. To get strong again."

"I'll never play baseball again, not with this hand."

"That's why you have to work to strengthen it," Mom said.

Mickey ignored her. He went on as if speaking to himself, "If I'm not a baseball player, who am I? What good am I? No good." He rolled over, scrunching into a ball. "Better if they send me away."

"No, you mustn't say that!" Mom cried silently, tears running down her face.

Could Mickey be right about his hand? Kenny wondered. *After all, he* had *pounded it pretty hard on the doorframe, hard enough to do damage to the wood. So it* was *a bad injury.*

But then he looked at Mickey's curled body, his lank hair, the exercise implements lying unused on the night table, and thought, *No.* Nurse Gregory had said that Mickey's hand had healed well, and Kenny believed her. And he knew, from when other Asahi players had broken bones, that if they followed their physical therapy, they could come back as good as new. No, this looked as if Mickey didn't *want* to get better.

Should I tell him about the baseball field? Kenny wondered. *After all, half the idea was to give him something to care about, and it might cheer him up.*

But he's so discouraged. Hearing about a baseball field that he can't play on might make him worse.

Besides, he reminded himself, *there* is *no baseball field. Not yet, anyway.*

He didn't say anything about it.

———

Kenny was so excited when another letter arrived from Susana.

July 20, 1942
Dear Kenny,

Well, I don't know if I really gave you the idea about the baseball field, but if you want to give me credit, I'll take it! It's brilliant! How is it coming? It sounds like a ton of work. Good thing you have Sammy to help. He sounds like a nice guy. And who knew Dai would turn out to be such a great worker?

You didn't mention Mickey. He must be excited about having baseball in the camp. Is he already planning to coach the teams when the field is ready?

Kenny sighed. If she only knew that Mickey wouldn't even get out of bed, let alone coach anybody.

The government people came around again. They seem to be making lists of what's left in everybody's house. I'll never tell where your stuff is, not even if they pull my fingernails out.

Love to Auntie Keiko and Mickey and Sally. Come
back soon, will you?

Your friend,
Susana

Kenny grabbed a sheet of paper.

Dear Susana,

What fingernails? You always chew them down to nothing.

He laughed out loud, picturing the look on her face.

Every couple of days, Tak and Jun came by to see how the
field was coming along. Each time, Tak jeered and Jun
laughed, like a faithful servant.

But one day Jun stared and pointed. "Hey, look at all
that ground, Tak! That's where first base would be. And
they're almost to second."

Tak snorted. "You mean the obstacle course?"

This time Jun didn't laugh. He came over to where Dai
had organized the piles. "That's an awful lot of bent nails,"
he said. "What are you going to do with them?"

Dai groaned. "We've got to straighten them out. But we just mess them up. And there's no time. I can barely keep up with the scraps these two workhorses keep handing me."

"I might be able to do it. I'm pretty good with my hands."

"Be my guest," Dai said, handing him the hammer and a bent nail.

Jun grabbed a short length of wood and laid the nail on it, kink upward. He tapped lightly, turned the nail, tapped again. He held up the nail. It was slightly crimped, but basically straight. "How's this?"

"You're hired!" Kenny shouted.

Jun laughed.

"Jun!" Tak called. "I thought you said this was stupid."

"That's what I thought." Jun picked up another nail. "But it's not. This field could happen. It *is* happening. I want to help."

"Suit yourself. I wouldn't play here if you paid me. When I was on the Clovers, we had a real field." Scowling, Tak stalked away.

Word spread in the camp. By now there were nearly fifty shacks built, and the population had grown to several hundred people. The workers saw what Kenny was doing, and piled up the scraps neatly rather than dumping them just anywhere. People started coming by to see the "baseball field." When they saw the neat piles that Dai had assembled, they started taking wood and nails to use in their cabins.

"This board'll make a good kitchen shelf," one woman said.

"If you split them thin, these cedar shakes make great kindling," another said.

"I can use a load of firewood," said a third.

Boys came with their parents to see what was going on, and they stayed to help. An older boy named Matsu turned out to be so dexterous that he joined Jun's nail-straightening crew, and the pile of straight nails grew nearly as fast as the stacks of wood. Kenny now had three assembly lines going, like the arms of an octopus, one stretching out into right field, one into center, and one into left. The materials were handed down each line from hand to hand, to a central point near where the pitcher's mound would be, and from there down a straight line from boy to boy, to Sammy, to Kenny, to Dai and Jun. Each day, the arms snaked deeper into the field. Each day, people came and took building supplies, and the piles shrank and grew, shrank and grew.

———

A familiar figure came to the edge of the field. It skulked along the third baseline, arms folded, face shadowed by a cap.

Kenny saw him. He didn't say anything.

Finally Tak ambled over. He shoved his hands into his pockets. "There's no one to play with. They're all here."

"Mmm-hmm," Kenny said noncommittally.

"So . . . I might as well help. There's nothing else to do."

Kenny didn't say what he was thinking: *Oh, I thought it was stupid.* Instead, he smiled. "That would be swell, Tak."

"So, where should I go?"

"Well, would you rather pick up stuff or help Dai and Jun sort it? Mind you, when you pick up the boards, you're bound to get splinters." He showed Tak his hands, which were a mess of scratches and cuts. He'd had so many splinters he barely noticed them anymore.

"I'm not afraid of a few splinters," Tak said quickly.

"Okay, then, why don't you join those boys out in center field? They can sure use the help."

"All right." Tak trotted away.

Kenny watched him go, shaking his head. Mentally, he started a letter to Susana: *Dear Susana, You won't believe this, but Tak Watanabe just took orders from* me!

But it wasn't just Tak. All day long, boys came to him:

"Kenny, where should I go?"

"Kenny, what should I do?"

Kenny wanted to laugh. *Who would believe that I'm the boss of the baseball field? No one back home, that's for sure.*

"Kenny? You there?"

Kenny snapped to, to find Sammy grinning at him, holding out a board.

"I am now," he said with a laugh, and passed it down the line.

19

After his mom visited Kenny in the field, he expected her to bug him about working so hard. But she didn't. He was saved by the O-Bon festival, the festival of the ancestors, held each year in early August. Mom was so busy getting ready for it that she seemed to forget to worry about him.

A few weeks earlier, Kenny had overheard her and Mrs. Watanabe talking about it over cups of tea.

"Remember how beautiful the Powell Street Grounds used to be, with the colored paper lanterns strung up all around?" Mom said with a sigh.

"And those beautiful origami flowers," Mrs. Watanabe added. "I must have folded them for weeks!"

"All the banners we sewed . . ."

"And all the dance practice we put in . . ."

"I remember your dancing, Fumiko-san," Mom said. "So light and graceful."

Kenny remembered, too. Tak's mother had seemed to float on air rather than on her feet, and her fan had seemed to flick from side to side without even a movement of her hand.

Mrs. Watanabe shook her head. "Oh no, not I. Just an average dancer—"

"Now, Fumiko," Mom scolded.

Mrs. Watanabe giggled. Then she sighed. "Ah, well, *shikata ga nai*. It can't be helped."

"What can't?"

"No O-Bon festival this year."

Mom gaped at her. "What do you mean? Of course we'll celebrate O-Bon. We have to."

"But how? We have no space. No lanterns. No origami flowers. No music. Nothing."

Mom got that look, the one that Kenny had come to recognize. Now that he thought about it, she didn't used to have it, back at home. It was only since they'd come to the camp that her face had taken on that look, her chin thrust forward and her eyes flashing. "We'll have to make do. We can't *not* honor the ancestors."

"Our group could dance, Mrs. Watanabe," Sally said.

Ever since Mrs. Watanabe had started teaching *odori* to

Sally, other girls had come forward, and now Mrs. Watanabe mentored a whole flock of young dancers. Kimonos waving and fans fluttering, they practiced in front of the shack. Sometimes Kenny had to weave his way through them, pushing dangling sleeves out of his face.

"But I haven't taught you the special Bon Odori dances," Mrs. Watanabe said.

"We could learn. Please?" Sally turned beseeching eyes to Mrs. Watanabe.

Kenny could see Tak's mother wavering. *She doesn't know it, but she's a goner.* "You'd have to work very hard . . ."

"Yes! Oh, thank you!"

Kenny exchanged a smile with Mom.

So it was that Mom became the chief of the O-Bon festival. She called a meeting of the women of the camp, and soon had them all organized. It was surprising how many people had managed to bring remnants of past festivals with them to New Denver. Some had brought lanterns. Others had brought the intricately folded paper flowers that they saved from year to year. Others had a stash of origami paper for making new ones.

Some people had brought their flutes and kotos, and they set to work, practicing the traditional songs. Mrs. Watanabe drilled the dancers every day. People unfolded their precious kimonos and hung them up to let the wrinkles settle.

Mom put them into groups, one group in charge of music, another in charge of refreshments. One to clear a space between the shacks, one to put up decorations. She sewed and mended, her mouth full of pins, scissors clicking.

All day people came running.

"Mrs. Sakamoto, do you think . . ."

"Will this do, Mrs. Sakamoto?"

Just like me and the field, Kenny thought wonderingly. *Who knew that two people who'd always followed others could become the ones in charge?*

On the evening of the festival, people gathered at the center of the camp. At first Kenny couldn't help but feel a pang of disappointment. Normally a raised wooden platform, the *yagura*, stood in the middle of the space, with the colorful lanterns and paper flowers strung up all around it. This year there was no *yagura*, and the lanterns and flowers were mounted haphazardly on the front of whatever shacks faced the open space.

But the dirt had been swept smooth, and many women and girls were in their kimonos, making the circle a kaleidoscope of pinks and blues and whites, flowered and checkered sleeves, silver and gold fans, ribbons trailing from piled-up hair. People fetched chairs and stumps for the older guests, and the babies sat or crawled in the dirt.

A flute played a plaintive melody, and then other instruments joined in, a steady, low drumbeat, the twang of the koto. Dusk deepened. Voices were lifted. Kenny added his voice to the ancient melody, calling to the ancestors. A chill went up his back.

Just before full darkness fell, the dancers, led by Mrs. Watanabe, formed a circle in the space. The musicians, in the center of the circle, started to play the Bon Odori music. Kenny's eyes swept the group. He looked right past Sally, then scanned back and stopped in amazement. She stood tall and assured. Her movements were precise and graceful. The long, full sleeves of her kimono belled out as her hands formed the shape of the sun, as she turned slowly in place, as she bent and straightened. Instead of sharp clicks on wood, her geta made soft thumps on the dirt. The candlelight peeking through the cutouts in the lanterns flickered on her black hair.

What a difference from when she danced with Gittie, Kenny thought, nearly laughing out loud at the memory of the two of them falling on top of each other. He remembered what Auntie Miriam had said, that Sally really had talent. He supposed Auntie Miriam was right. A pang gripped him. Susana. Auntie Miriam and Uncle Jake. Gittie. *If only Auntie Miriam could be here to say "I told you so." If only Susana could be here to laugh with me, to be proud with me.*

Then a deeper pang hit. *Dad. Is he celebrating O-Bon in his road camp tonight? Is he missing us? Is he thinking of his parents, gone these many years? Does he have music, and lanterns, and flowers, or just darkness and the cold, hard ground?*

Kenny's eyes filled with tears.

And what about Mickey? Does he even know it's O-Bon? Is he remembering the music? Or is he lying in his hospital room, thinking of nothing?

Kenny came back to himself. O-Bon was for honoring the ancestors. He bowed and said a little prayer for Dad's parents, who had died, and another prayer for Mom's parents in Japan, to keep them safe in the midst of war, and another for all his ancestors, those he knew and those he didn't know, thanking them for the lives they had lived, leading straight to him.

The dance ended. People plucked the lanterns from the walls and, walking single file, carried them in a long flickering line down to the lake. As they walked past, many bowed to Mom and murmured their thanks. Even in the dark, Kenny could see her face flush with pride.

At the lakeshore, Kenny placed his lantern on the water and gave it a little push. Mom drew him near and put her other arm around Sally. Together, silently, they watched the lanterns drift out on the lake, sometimes wobbling on small waves, sometimes zooming ahead on a gust of wind.

The lights grew dimmer.

"The ancestors are happy," Mom whispered.

20

One day in mid-August, as Kenny was heading out the door to go to the field, Mom called him back. "Kenny, come here. You need to try on your clothes for school."

"School?" Kenny said, horrified.

"Yes, school. Don't you know that Mrs. Kimura and Nakata-sensei have arranged everything? You'll start after Labor Day, just like normal."

In the back of his mind, Kenny had known that school was in the works. He knew that Dai's mother had finally convinced Mr. Richardson to open a school for the younger children and that, with the help of Nakata-sensei, she'd been rounding up books, finding teachers among the camp population and converting one of the shacks for use as a schoolhouse. But Kenny, occupied with the field, had put it out of his mind. *Not yet!* he thought. *The field! Baseball!*

"Can't I do it later, Mom?"

"Kenji Sakamoto . . ."

"Oh, all right."

Mom took a pair of trousers down from the shelf in the bedroom. A few weeks earlier, when some men had come to the field for building materials, they'd been so impressed with what Kenny was doing that they'd offered to build the Sakamotos shelves. Mom had sewn curtains to cover them, and now Kenny didn't have to dig in the suitcase when he needed clothes.

He took off his shorts and put on the trousers. He felt air around his ankles and looked down. His anklebones were sticking out.

"Too short," Mom said, frowning. "Try these ones."

The second pair was too short as well.

Kenny slipped on a long-sleeved button-down shirt. His wrists protruded from the cuffs.

"You've grown," Mom said in dismay. "Nothing fits."

"I guess I have," Kenny said cheerfully. *Finally I'm not a runt anymore.*

Mom looked at him with a wondering expression. "And you're so brown and strong-looking, and you look so well."

"Let me see," Kenny said. He twisted to see himself in the tiny mirror hanging over the shelf. He *had* changed.

His face was thinner. There was definition around his cheekbones. His skin was tanned. He looked down. His body was slimmer. Longer.

Mom clutched Kenny's arm. "Kenny! How is your heart? Oh, Lord, I've been so preoccupied I haven't been paying attention. Are you all right? You're not overdoing it, are you?"

"I'm fine, Mom." As he said it, Kenny realized that it was true. He hadn't been paying attention to his heart either. In fact, he'd been so busy over the last several weeks, with the field, and with his chores, and with helping Mom, and with walking the three miles into town to see Mickey and the three miles back again, that he'd forgotten all about it. He couldn't remember the last time he'd felt it beat fast. He no longer had to stop while carrying the water buckets up the hill, or take breaks from hauling wood scraps on the "assembly line."

Mom gave him an appraising look. "You *look* fine."

"I am. I really am. I think—" He stopped. "You know, Dr. Hayakawa didn't say that I *had* a heart murmur. He only said he thought I did. Remember?"

Mom nodded uncertainly.

"He said, 'It may be serious. It might mean nothing.' Maybe it really was nothing. Or maybe it somehow got better." He didn't know if that was possible. But he felt that way. Strong. Normal.

"It's a miracle," Mom said under her breath. Her eyes glistened.

Kenny squirmed. "Aw, Mom, don't go all weepy on me." Quickly he changed back into his shorts. "Here," he said, handing her the trousers and shirt. "See you at lunchtime!"

The next day, Kenny and Mom set off for New Denver to see Mickey. Mom carried the food basket, and Kenny held a large paper bag. Before they reached the edge of the camp, he ducked into the administrator's office. "Uh, Constable Murphy, could I talk to you for a minute?"

Mr. Richardson shot Kenny a dirty look, as if to say, *What could the likes of you have to say to an officer of the law?* But Constable Murphy said, "Sure," and slipped outside. Kenny whispered something. Constable Murphy thought for a moment. Then he nodded. "Yes, that would be fair."

"Thank you, sir."

Mom looked at him curiously, but she didn't ask. As they walked, Kenny debated with himself about whether to show Mickey what was in the bag. *Only if he's still really down in the dumps*, he decided. *Only if I'm desperate.*

At the hospital, there was no change. Nurse Gregory told them that the doctor still refused to discharge Mickey. Not only was his hand weak, but he had lost so much weight that he needed to build his strength back up.

Mickey was lying on his bed. His hair was disheveled. His shoulder blades poked out from his shirt. The rubber ball, elastic band and barbell were coated with dust.

Mom sank onto the bed beside him with a deep sigh. "Oh, Mickey."

"Mom, why do you come? I don't deserve your company. I'm—what did that man call me?—a troublemaker."

"No, you're not, and you mustn't say so," Mom said. "You did a bad thing, yes, but you're a good boy."

"Don't listen to what Mr. Richardson says, Mickey," Kenny said. "He's just an old grump."

Mickey curled up with his back to them. "I've shamed you so, I would only bring more disgrace on you by showing my face in the camp."

"That's not true," Mom said. "Everyone's forgotten. All you have to do is get better and come home."

"Mom's right, Mickey," Kenny said. "We need you."

"No one needs me. I'm an outcast."

Kenny was dismayed. Mickey was worse than ever. Kenny's hands tightened on the bag.

Should I?

It might make Mickey more upset.

It might work.

He opened the bag and placed Mickey's Asahi shirt, pants and cap on the bed in front of him.

Mickey gasped, and Kenny realized that Mickey never knew Kenny had packed it. Mickey clutched the uniform to his body. His body trembled. Kenny could tell he was struggling not to cry. A sob escaped him. Then Mickey was bawling. "I've disgraced my uniform," he choked out. "I don't deserve to call myself an Asahi."

Kenny waited. Finally Mickey's sobs subsided. Kenny put his hand on Mickey's shoulder. "You're still an Asahi, Mickey. You always will be."

Mickey shook his head. "Baseball is over."

"That's where you're wrong."

"What?" Mickey rolled over and sat up, clutching the damp uniform. He stared at Kenny. "What do you mean?"

"Baseball isn't over. It's just beginning. I wasn't going to tell you this yet, but, well . . ."

Kenny told him about the field. About how the boys had come to help, one at a time. About how they had carted load after load of debris from the vacant lot. About how it was almost clear. Almost a baseball field.

"And it was all Kenny's idea," Mom told Mickey proudly.

Kenny looked at her in amazement.

Mickey's face had grown lighter as he'd listened. But now it darkened again. "I damaged the cabin. I'm still in trouble."

"No!" Kenny said loudly, and Mickey's head snapped up. "That's what I'm trying to tell you. Constable Murphy said you can make amends for what you did by coaching the boys in baseball."

Mickey opened his mouth, but Kenny held up his hand, rushing on before Mickey could say no. "Listen to me. They all want you. Half the kids in camp have asked me if you'll coach them. They need you. *I* need you. Please, Mickey."

Mickey didn't say anything for a moment. Then, "He really said that? Constable Murphy?"

"Yes."

A silence. "And you're sure about the boys? They won't . . . you know . . . ?"

"I swear to you. All you have to do is work on your hand. Get it better."

"And eat!" Mom added.

Mickey sat up a little straighter. He picked up the rubber ball and gave it a squeeze.

Once they got outside, Mom pulled Kenny to a stop. "So that's what you were whispering about with Constable Murphy."

Kenny shrugged. "I was desperate. It was the only thing I could think of."

Mom crushed Kenny to her chest. "My boy. My Kenji." Then she held him away with a laugh. "I should have known you were up to something."

21

Kenny stood where home plate would be, hands on hips, and surveyed the field. It was clear. All the scraps and pieces of wood had been removed. Behind him, Dai's piles were as neat as ever. Jun had found a wooden box with inner compartments, like a cutlery drawer, and he and Matsu had sorted straightened nails of different lengths into the sections, so that when people came they could choose the exact nails they needed. People called the area beside the field "Sakamoto's Hardware Store" and jokingly told Kenny he should go into business.

But the field was a lumpy, bumpy mess. Boulders were wedged into the dirt. Weeds and thistles poked up everywhere. Between left field and center field, a tree stump protruded several inches above the ground, its roots snaking in every direction. The land closest to the creek was covered by a tangle of blackberry vines.

Kenny sighed. The field might be free of debris, but it was still going to take a lot of work to get it into shape for baseball. He and the boys couldn't dig up the stump and flatten the ground. It would take a machine to do that. And the field needed a backstop, and bases, and base paths.

Kenny hated to go begging to Mr. Richardson, but he couldn't think of anything else. He dragged himself over to the camp supervisor's office.

Mr. Richardson was on the telephone, and while Kenny waited, he looked around the office. He'd noticed Mr. Richardson's crowded desk before, but now he really saw it. Folders were piled high, threatening to topple over. Rolled-up building plans lined one edge of the desk. Behind the desk a small bookshelf was full, with papers stacked on top of it.

An idea struck. When Mr. Richardson got off the telephone and said, "Yes, what is it?" Kenny smiled. "Good morning, sir. The field is all clear, and we wanted to thank you. Perhaps you and Constable Murphy would like to come out and see it?"

Constable Murphy shot Kenny a curious look. Kenny just hoped he'd pick up the hint.

Several of the boys were at the field when the three of them arrived. Some looked proud. Others looked nervous. Everyone knew how hard Mr. Richardson was to please.

To their surprise, though, Mr. Richardson nodded. "Very good." He pointed to the piles of wood and the box of nails. "Neat. Tidy. I must say I'm surprised. Pleasantly surprised."

Kenny's mouth fell open. "Thank you, sir," he said.

"I'll say," Constable Murphy said with a laugh. "Why, you boys have done a marvelous job, and, from what I hear, people in the camp feel very grateful for the supplies."

"Yes, sir."

"It's still a bit rough, though, Mr. Richardson, sir," Kenny pointed out. "We can't really play on it yet."

"You can't expect the Powell Street Grounds!" Mr. Richardson snapped.

"No, of course not," Kenny said. He swallowed. "But I was wondering if we could make a deal."

"A deal?" Mr. Richardson thundered. "What kind of deal would you have to make with me?"

Kenny cringed, but was relieved when he heard a chuckle from Constable Murphy. "What I mean, sir, is that I've noticed that you could use a new bookshelf in your office."

Kenny caught a quick nod from Dai. His friend had figured out where he was going. "Yes, sir, we have all this terrific wood here," Dai said.

"And all these nails," Jun added, jumping in.

"And we'd be happy to build it for you," Kenny said, hoping there was someone among the boys who knew how to do such a thing.

Constable Murphy laughed. "I think what these boys are trying to say, Harley, is that they'll help you deal with your office overload if you help them finish the field. Bring in a machine to level things out, put up a backstop. Is that it, Kenny?"

"Yes, sir."

"Why, of all the—"

"Hold on now, Harley," Constable Murphy said. "Look how hard they worked. And just think, this project has kept all these boys out of trouble."

"Hmm . . ."

"And the salvage operation has saved the government money on building supplies that didn't have to be purchased."

"Hmm . . ."

"And from what I hear, these Japanese boys are pretty

good ballplayers. We could get a swell competition going with the town team."

"Well—" beside him, Kenny sensed the sudden hush as all the boys held their breath. "All right. We can spare some men and equipment. But no mollycoddling. We're not running a charity here."

"Of course not, sir. Thank you, sir," Kenny said, and the other boys echoed his words.

Mr. Richardson turned to go. Constable Murphy winked at Kenny, then followed.

The boys swarmed Kenny. "Way to go, Kenny!"

He walked home with his friends' arms slung around him.

The next day, a huge machine arrived. It dug up the boulders and pushed them off the field. A man came with a saw and cut the tree stump flush with the ground. Another man used a pickax to dig up the blackberry roots. Once the rocks and vines were gone, the machine went back and forth across the field, pushing the dirt with a long, flat blade, filling in holes and leveling out humps.

Kenny and the other boys stood and watched, shouting over the roar of the motor.

"Look at that boulder roll like a marble!"

"That machine just pulled up those roots like they were threads!"

The men brought eight-foot-long boards and rolls of chicken wire. They dug holes behind home plate, sank the bottoms of the boards, built a crosswise scaffold and attached the chicken wire to form a backstop.

Tak and Sammy scrounged four empty rice sacks and filled them with gravel. Sammy stole his mother's needle and thread and, to the teasing of the other boys, sewed them up.

Dai measured the exact distances and angles, and the bases were put in place. Kenny stood there, wondering how they were going to mark the base paths. Since there wasn't any chalk in the camp, he supposed they'd have to draw lines in the dirt with a stick.

Just then one of the workers came back. His jacket bulged. "Don't tell Mr. R., but I just happened to borrow this from the clubhouse by the provincial government building." He opened his jacket and slipped Kenny a cloth bag. Kenny peeked inside. Chalk!

"Thanks, sir!"

The man winked and walked away.

———

Jun and Matsu, who were so clever with their hands, offered to build the bookshelf. Dai measured the boards, Tak cut them, Kenny sanded them, and Jun and Matsu put it all together. The five boys even helped Mr. Richardson load his folders and papers onto the shelves.

Mr. Richardson stood back and regarded his new bookshelf. He swept his hand over his bare desk. "Very handsome. Quite an improvement." He cleared his throat. "Thank you."

The boys exchanged smiles as they piled out the door.

A truck rumbled into the camp and stopped at the camp supervisor's office. Kenny, waiting at the entrance with Mom and Sally, squeezed Mom's hand.

Constable Murphy and Mickey got out. Mickey glanced at them, then looked down as he followed Constable Murphy into the building. Kenny could hear Mr. Richardson's lecturing tones, Mickey's quiet replies. Then Mickey and Constable Murphy came out.

Mom's body leaned toward Mickey; Kenny felt her trembling as she held herself back. Instead, she held out her hands to Constable Murphy. "Thank you, sir."

"Thank me? For what, ma'am?"

"For not sending my son away. For taking care of him."

"Oh, that's all right. I could tell he was a good boy. Besides," Constable Murphy said with a laugh, "I want to challenge him to a baseball game. I hear he's pretty talented."

"He's the best!" Kenny said.

That drew a smile from Mickey.

They left Constable Murphy and made their way back to the cabin, Sally clinging to one of Mickey's hands and Mom to the other. Walking beside them, Kenny could see that Mickey's face was tense and his shoulders were hunched. Every time they passed someone, Mickey lowered his eyes.

Nakata-sensei hurried over and pumped Mickey's hand. "Welcome home, Mitsuo. So good to have you back."

"Thank you, Sensei," Mickey whispered.

A group of boys who had helped on the field trailed behind the Sakamotos. Kenny heard a whisper. "Is that Kenny's big brother? The Asahi?"

"Yeah, that's him," another boy answered.

"Wow."

A cute older girl, whom Kenny recognized from Sally's dance group, passed by. Sally shrieked. "Kiyo! Mickey's home!"

The girl paused. "So you're the famous big brother," she said, dimples flashing.

Mickey blushed, and everybody laughed.

By the time they got to the cabin, Mickey looked more relaxed. Still, as he went inside, he glanced at the doorframe, as if afraid to see signs of where he'd bashed it.

He sat Mom down and knelt before her. Head bowed, he said, "*Okaasan*, I am truly sorry for the pain I caused you. Please forgive me."

Mom stroked his black hair. "There is no need to ask, Mitsuo. You are my son."

Mickey heaved a trembling sigh. When he stood up, the tension had left his face.

Kenny was longing to show Mickey the field, but first Mom had to feed him. Mickey had gained a few pounds, but he was still thin. Bowl after bowl she placed on the table: rice, miso soup made from her precious and dwindling supply of miso paste, *hiya yakko* and steamed greens, mostly wild mustard and dandelion greens gathered from the surrounding woods. Then Sally had to show him all her new things: the silver and red fan that Mrs. Watanabe had given her, and the hook where her kimono hung, and the picture she'd drawn of Dad, which Mom had taped up, and the tissue paper someone had given her to wrap her obi in, which she carefully reused every time she put the obi away.

Mickey dutifully exclaimed over everything, while Kenny fidgeted beside him. Finally Mickey turned to him. "Okay, Kenny, let's see this famous field of yours."

"Holy cow," Mickey said.

They stood at home plate. Mickey looked past first base to right field, across center, to left field and third base. He strolled out to the pitcher's mound and looked back toward home.

"I can't believe it, Kenny. How on earth did you . . . ?"

"All the fellas helped. And Mr. Richardson had the field leveled and the backstop built. But it was really Constable Murphy. He made Mr. Richardson do it."

Mickey shook his head. "It's amazing. *You're* amazing, Kenny."

"No, I'm not. I—"

Mickey waved a hand, cutting him off. He swallowed, once, twice. He looked like he wanted to say something, but nothing came out. Finally, "I don't know what I would have done—" His voice cracked. He grabbed Kenny in a hug.

Kenny felt his cheeks get hot. "It wasn't me. You came around—"

Mickey held him at arm's length. "No. I'd still be in there if you hadn't . . . hadn't done this. Done everything."

Kenny squirmed. "I'm just glad you're here."

"Me, too." Mickey quickly wiped his eyes, then grinned. "I'm itching to play. Come on, let's have a catch." He trotted back toward home plate and picked up his glove.

"Is your hand better?" Kenny asked.

Mickey flexed his fingers. "Not 100 percent, but pretty close. I'm working on it. But the rest of me"—he windmilled his arms—"is really out of shape. Go easy on me, will you?"

"Yeah, sure, *I'll* go easy on *you*," Kenny said with a laugh.

Mickey suddenly became serious. "Wait a minute. I shouldn't be pushing you. Are you—can you do this, Kenny?"

Kenny nodded. "I'm okay. I feel fine."

Mickey peered at him. "You look okay. Heck, Kenny, you look great. You've grown, and you look—I don't know—different."

"All my clothes are too small."

"Still, you shouldn't overdo it."

"Mickey, I've been hauling lumber for the last month."

Mickey nodded. "So you have. But you'll tell me if you feel tired, right?"

"*Mickey.*"

"Okay, okay," Mickey said with a laugh. He threw the ball in a high arc. Kenny ran back, put up his glove—and caught it.

22

First came Dai and Jun. Then Tak and Sammy. Then other boys in ones and twos, threes and fours, with gloves and balls and one or two precious bats that had been squeezed into the family luggage. Eight-year-olds, fourteen-year-olds and everyone in between.

"Can I play?"

"Is there a team?"

"Will you coach me?"

"Can I play?"

At first, Kenny noticed, Mickey was a bit standoffish. Although he shook hands with each new boy that Kenny introduced, he quickly looked down in the direction of his feet.

But then the boys started firing questions at him.

"When do you bring the bat around when you're bunting?"

Mickey looked up. "Right away. As soon as the ball leaves the pitcher's hand."

"How do you get under a high fly ball?"

A smile broke out. "Keep your eye on it all the way. It's easy, really. Just takes practice."

"Easy for you, maybe," Dai said, and everybody laughed.

"How about that hit you made in the final. Can you teach me to hit like that?" Tak asked.

"Good luck," Sammy said.

"Any tips for being a better shortstop?" someone asked.

"Whoa, whoa," Mickey said with a chuckle. "Let's get warmed up first."

Soon he had the boys organized in pairs, throwing the ball back and forth. He went down the line, correcting an arm motion here, a foot position there. Then he sent groups of boys out into the field and, as he hit fly balls and grounders, had them practice fielding drills, first base to second to third, shortstop to home, center field to second, left field to third base to home.

Kenny watched as Mickey reared back to throw, demonstrating the proper technique for one boy who looked stiff and hesitant. Mickey's arm zipped around like the end of a whip, with that magic snap he used to have, and the ball zinged straight and true as if on an invisible line.

"Did you see that?" Sammy whispered to Jun. Jun just shook his head in wonderment. Kenny's chest swelled.

So many boys showed up that there were enough for two teams. Matsu turned out to be a terrific ball player, and patient, too, so Mickey asked him to coach the other team. Matsu, his face coloring, said, "Me?" Then, "Sure!" They divided the boys, putting a range of younger and older, more talented and less skilled players on each team. Then, with the teams established, Mickey and Matsu planned a schedule of practices, with the first game to be played in about a week's time.

Kenny was delighted to be on the same team as Dai and Jun. But when his teammates voted him captain, Kenny held up his hands. "I shouldn't be captain. I'm not even that good. Lots of you fellas are better than me." *All of you, in fact.*

"We want Kenny. We want Kenny," chanted the players.

Jun slapped him on the back. "Face it, pal. You're it."

Kenny blushed. "Thanks, fellas." But all he could think was *I hope I don't let you down.*

The teams chose names. Tak's team, of which he was captain, called themselves the Nippons. *It's a clever name,* Kenny thought, harking back to the original Japanese Canadian team that had given way to the Asahis.

Kenny's team sat in a circle behind the backstop.

"How about the Sluggers?" a little boy suggested, flexing his skinny arm, and everybody laughed.

"The Emperors?"

"The Eagles?"

"The Giants?"

The Asahis buzzed around in Kenny's brain. But of course they couldn't use that. They weren't the Asahis. No one else could be.

But what if they played off the name? *Asahi* meant *morning sun.* "How about the Nichis?" he said.

"The what?" one boy asked.

Dai nodded. "I get it. *Nichi* means *sun,*" he explained to the boy. "So it's like *asahi,* but it's not a straight copy."

"Good one, Kenny," Jun said.

Kenny grinned. "Like the sun, we're rising."

"We're shining."

"We're bright."

"Go, Nichis!" Jun shouted, and everyone clapped.

"Okay," Kenny said. "We don't have uniforms, but see if your mother will let you draw a yellow sun on a T-shirt. And remember, we only have half a dozen more practices, and then the first game is the day after that. Labor Day."

"And then it's school," Dai said.

"Don't say that!" all the boys yelled.

Mom said Kenny could use one of his old, stained T-shirts for a uniform shirt. He pilfered a yellow crayon from Sally and drew a sun on the left breast, coloring it in as hard as he could. He pulled on the shirt and stood on a chair to look in the small mirror over the clothing shelf. The sun looked pale and pathetic, but it was the best he could do.

In the morning, he found the shirt draped over the stool in the corner of the bedroom. At first he thought that Mom must have thrown out the one he'd colored and substituted another one. This one had been decorated with a bright yellow cloth sun, with spiky rays coming out of it. The fabric had been fastened to the T-shirt with small, neat stitches.

Mom lifted her head from the pillow.

"You did this, Mom?"

She smiled.

"Thanks." Then he noticed the small letter *C* for *Captain* embroidered over the right breast. "Thanks!"

He pulled the shirt on over his pajamas and looked in the mirror. The sun shone bright and golden from his chest.

A thought struck. *I'm captain. The boys are going to be depending on me.* His stomach clenched.

Later that day, after baseball practice, he waited until all the boys had left before pulling his brother aside. "Uh, Mickey?"

"Yeah?"

"It's great that you're coaching—"

"And you know what, Kenny? I really don't mind. I mean, I never thought I'd *coach*. I always thought of myself as a player. But here we are, and they're good kids, and—"

"Yeah, that's true, they are—"

"And besides—" Mickey's voice lowered "—it gives me a way to, well . . . make it up to people. It was so kind of Constable Murphy to let me pay it off this way. And I know it was your idea, Kenny."

"Yeah, but—"

"No buts. I appreciate it."

"Mickey!" Kenny yelled.

His brother looked at him in surprise. "What?"

"I'm trying to ask you something."

"Oh. What?"

"Would you train me?"

"Isn't that what we were just doing?"

"No, I mean, would you train *me*. Separately."

"What for? You looked all right out there. I don't think you need special coaching, like before."

Kenny blushed. He didn't want to say what he really meant—that he was afraid to look bad in front of the other boys. Oh, sure, he'd improved, he knew that. He wasn't a total klutz anymore, and he was a lot stronger and surer on his feet. He knew how to get under a ball. He could fire back a grounder and almost hit his target. He didn't get so tired—at least, no more tired than the other boys.

But I'm still not good. *I don't have baseball in my muscles, like the other boys do. I don't have the moves.*

He'd felt as if he was *beginning* to get it, back when Mickey was training him in Vancouver, but then all of that had been swept away.

Strange, he thought. *Back then, no one expected me to be able to do anything, so even if I'd flubbed the Clovers' tryouts, it wouldn't have been such a disgrace. But now people know me. They think I'm some big hero. They expect me to do great things. And if I mess up, it'll be worse.*

"Please?"

Mickey looked at him. "Sure, Kenny."

Kenny breathed a sigh of relief.

He found a patch of land near the lake that was screened by trees, and persuaded Mickey to come out with him early in the morning.

"What do you want to work on?"

"Hitting."

"Okay. Remember what I told you before?"

"Swing level and keep my eye on the ball."

But no matter how many times Mickey demonstrated, or how many times Kenny practiced, he just couldn't hit. He knew what he had to do. He saw the ball come in. His arms and shoulders were stronger than before, and the bat didn't wobble like it had in the fall. But he either missed the ball or tapped soft, pathetic hits that rolled a few feet and died in the dirt.

"Put your shoulders into it," Mickey said.

"Turn your hips when you swing the bat."

"Pivot faster on your back foot."

"Don't try to clobber the ball. Just meet it."

Kenny tried them all. He hit the same feeble hits. He struck out.

He threw the bat in the dirt.

I'm going to look like a fool at the plate.

And if you can't hit, what good are you?

23

One day in late August, practicing drills with the other boys, Kenny heard the sound of a truck rumbling into the camp. He didn't pay it any mind. Trucks were always coming and going.

But a few minutes later, he began to hear cries.

"Father!"

"*Otousan!*"

"Dad!"

Kenny and Mickey looked at one another. They, and all the other boys, dropped their gloves and ran. Along the way, they were joined by families streaming from their shacks, mothers with babies, little kids, old people hobbling along.

"What is it?" people called.

"Who's there?"

Kenny and Mickey ran to the shack and grabbed Mom and Sally.

The truck had come to a stop in a cloud of dust near the camp supervisor's office. Kenny recognized that truck—it was the one with the high wooden slats, the one that had brought him and his family to the camp so many weeks ago.

The bed of the truck was crowded with men. Tired-looking men with crushed caps. Men carrying bundles. Men peering over the slats at the women and children who were running toward them. Men with outstretched arms, with smiles.

"What . . . ? Who . . . ?" Kenny asked a woman next to him.

"Haven't you heard? They're letting the men from the road camps rejoin their families."

"They are?" *Dad could be back!* "Where is this truck from, do you know?"

The woman shrugged. "Somewhere up north, I heard."

Revelstoke was north. North of New Denver, anyway. Kenny took Mom's hand and pushed through the crowd of people gathered around the truck. All around him he saw hugs, heard shrieks of joy. Tears flowed. People weren't even ashamed to cry in public.

"Father!"

"Mats, is that you?"

Is he here? Oh, please, let him be here.

Kenny saw Dai enfolded in his father's arms. Sammy, too. Jun, like Kenny, was squirming through the crowd with his mother, searching.

He wasn't there. Kenny had circled all the way around the truck, and he met Mickey, holding Sally in his arms, coming back the other way. The brothers shook their heads at one another. Mom's shoulders slumped.

"Maybe the next one, Mom," Kenny said as they started walking back to the cabin, surrounded by happy families with arms linked, and unhappy ones trudging back alone.

Mom brightened. "Maybe."

The next day, a crew of workers showed up at the shack. For several days they had been going from shack to shack, unrolling lengths of tar paper and stapling them to the inner walls in preparation for winter. They arrived with their rolls and staplers just as Kenny and Mickey were about to go to their secret spot to practice.

"Where do you two think you're going?" Mom said.

"Uh . . . out."

Mom shook her head. "We have to take everything down from the shelves. You're not going anywhere."

But, Mom, I need practice, Kenny wanted to say. *The first game is coming up on Labor Day. Only five days away. And I can't hit.*

Two hours later, after everything had been taken down and put back up again, it was too late for the private practice. Kenny's stomach fluttered.

The next day, the brothers were slipping out when Mom stopped them. "I need you to go out into the woods," she said.

Not again! Another day missed. Four days till the game.

But Kenny held his tongue. He knew that this foraging trip was important. Most of the camp residents had long ago run out of their Japanese staples, and, although the Red Cross had visited the camp and distributed rice and shoyu, people missed their *udon* and their *tsuke-mono*, their nori and their rice crackers. One store in town had begun to stock Japanese foods, but there was little choice and the prices were high. Nakata-sensei had asked Mr. Richardson if people could go across the lake to forage for wild plants and herbs to put by for winter, and he had given permission. Citizens of New Denver had even loaned their rowboats for the trip.

"You and Mickey go. Bring back as much as you can," Mom said.

Kenny glanced at Mickey. His glove was in his hand, and he looked like he wanted to protest. He closed his mouth. Kenny grinned. *At least we're in it together.*

He never would have admitted it, but it was a lovely trip. The mist that covered the lake was just starting to lift as he and Mickey climbed into a rowboat. The last tendrils of fog swirled past them as they skimmed along the surface, the only sounds the splash of the oars, the cry of a loon, the drumming of a woodpecker in the distant woods. On the other side, they hiked up ravines and, copying Matsu—who, it turned out, knew the back woods—filled bags with mushrooms, wild garlic, mint, the last of the huckleberries and blackberries.

"Now can we go?" Kenny asked when he and Mickey got back.

"Not yet," Mom said. "Help me rig up a drying rack."

Mickey quickly nailed together a wooden frame, and Kenny attached a piece of loosely woven cloth to it. Mickey suspended the rack above the cookstove.

"Now?" Kenny said.

"What's keeping you?" Mom gave his bottom a smack.

"Mom!" With a laugh, Kenny tore out.

Meanwhile, Mrs. Kimura, Dai's mother, was preparing to open the school in an empty shack. Her squad of teachers, some of whom were actual teachers and some of whom were high school students, like Kiyo, Sally's dancer friend, roamed through the camp collecting books and pencils, workbooks and paper. The older boys, including Mickey, were pressed into building benches and installing a woodstove in the shack for colder weather. That used up another day.

The preparations for school reminded Mom that Kenny needed new school clothes. She and some other women organized a clothing exchange, where families brought clothing that their older children had outgrown, and younger children tried them on, meanwhile passing on their own too-small clothes. Mom rigged up two change rooms with curtains, one for boys and one for girls, and a group of women sat by with needles and thread, taking up hems or letting them down, shortening cuffs, putting in darts, sewing on extra buttons or buckles. Kenny was glad to pass on his too-short pants and too-tight shirts to Jun, who was smaller than he was, and even more glad to receive pants and shirts from Matsu. He was tall and athletic, and Kenny was proud to be inheriting his clothes. The trousers needed shortening, though, and Kenny chafed while Mom pinned up the cuffs.

"Stop wiggling, Kenny," she scolded.

Kenny tried. But every hour that ticked by was time spent not practicing. Time he needed to improve. He swiveled his head, trying to catch Mickey's eye, to send the message that he would be finished in a minute, and could they please cram in just one more session?

"Kenny, stand still!"

On the last day before the game, Kenny and Mickey finally managed to get away early in the morning. Mickey looked at the ground. "Uh, Kenny . . . I've been thinking."

"Yeah?"

"Well, when it comes to hitting—" Mickey began.

"I stink."

"I wouldn't put it that way."

"I would." Kenny could see it all now. *Strikeout after lousy hit after strikeout. Hoots and laughter. "Why'd we make* him *captain?" his teammates would whisper.*

"So, let's go back to bunting. You weren't bad at that before."

"Well, maybe. Okay." *Can't be any worse, that's for sure.*

He practiced the motion, pivot and crouch, pivot and crouch. His body remembered. The bat felt lighter in his hands.

Mickey threw. Kenny connected. The ball didn't go far; it would have been an easy pickup for the catcher, and, in a real game, Kenny would have been thrown out.

"See?" Mickey said.

It was a fluke, Kenny told himself.

His next bunt went farther, landing halfway to the pitcher's mound.

"That's it. You're getting it."

Kenny tried to damp it down, but a ray of hope rose all the same. He'd *felt* where to put the bat, just as he had in Vancouver.

Of course, he told himself, bunting wasn't the same as hitting. It didn't have the glamor. He'd much rather have been able to stand at the plate and whack a homer, or even just a line drive. He'd rather hear the crack of the ball hitting the bat on a sharp hit than the soft pop of a bunt.

But then, squaring off on the next pitch, Kenny thought of his favorite Asahi player, Junji Ito. The King of Bunting had been able to place his bunts with the precision of a surgeon, making an incision here, a cut there. And he wasn't the only one. Many Asahi players had excelled at bunting. Teams had won entire games without a single hit, securing victory by playing "brain ball" with outstanding fielding, base running and bunting. And fans had celebrated those bunters, cheering just as loudly as they did for the great hitters.

Kenny thrust out the bat. The ball connected and ricocheted to the sweet zone between the pitcher, the catcher and the shortstop.

Maybe, just maybe, I won't be a total flop at the plate after all.

24

Kenny awoke. He yawned and stretched on his bed-roll. The drowsy part of his brain told him that there was something he was supposed to remember. *What is it?* He couldn't think. *Oh well.* He rolled over to catch a few more minutes of sleep—

The game!

Today was the game. The Nichis versus the Nippons. And not just the first game at the internment camp, but Kenny's first game ever.

He sat bolt upright. His stomach clenched. His heart beat fast. He didn't know if he was more nervous or excited. Both, he decided.

He slid out of bed. He put on his uniform shirt. Knowing that the yellow sun was over his heart made him feel a little bit better. He had his uniform. He had his team. He had Mickey cheering him on.

At breakfast, he scooped up a spoonful of oatmeal, then put the spoon down.

"Kenny, eat. You need your energy," Mom said.

Kenny shook his head. The only consolation was that Tak wasn't able to eat anything either. The other boy looked like he wanted to throw up.

"Good luck, Tak," Kenny said.

"Good luck, Kenny."

As Kenny and Mickey headed out the door for the field, boys streamed in from all directions. And not just players. Sisters and brothers, parents and grandparents, even people who had no connection to the teams. This game had been the talk of the camp for days. The whole community was coming. Mom and Sally would be along soon.

"Pretty evenly matched," Kenny heard.

"A miracle that we have a field in the first place . . ."

"Good pitching duel . . ."

Jun ran up in his yellow-crayoned shirt. "Hey, Kenny, did you sleep? I couldn't even sleep I was so excited."

Kenny laughed.

They were almost at the field when he heard the sound of a truck. He and Mickey looked at each other. They dropped their gloves and ran. "Mom! Sally! Another truck is here," they yelled, poking their heads in at the shack door.

Mom, in her apron, and Sally, in her pajamas, joined them in running down the path. Mom pulled at her apron strings. "I don't want him to see me like this."

"Mom!" Kenny laughed, tugging her along.

There were fewer people crowded around the truck this time, since many families had already been reunited. Still, there was a crush of people, and Kenny had to squeeze through, Mom in tow, to get a look at the men climbing down from the truck.

Is that him? No, just a man with a similar build.

Kenny saw Jun in the arms of a man with the same short, wiry stature. He smiled at his friend and kept searching.

"Keiko!" someone yelled, and Kenny and Mom snapped their heads around. But it was another man hugging another Keiko.

Mickey and Sally squeezed in beside Kenny and Mom. "Any sign of him?" Mickey asked.

"No," Kenny said.

Wait. A man was pushing toward them. The set of his shoulders was familiar, though the black hair was threaded with gray.

"Dad!"

The next thing Kenny knew, he, Mom, Mickey and Sally were encircled in Dad's arms.

"Hiroshi!" Mom wept. "Hiroshi!"

"Keiko . . . Keiko . . ."

"Daddy!" Sally jumped into his arms, legs around his waist.

Dad staggered back a step, laughing and crying at once. "Easy does it. My God, Sally, how you've grown!" He put her down and crushed Kenny and Mickey to him, one in each arm. "My sons."

Kenny cried against Dad's chest, and he didn't care who saw. Mickey did, too. Dad looked tired. His face was more lined. But he still had his familiar smell, of green tea and aftershave. Kenny breathed it in.

Finally Dad released them. He stepped back. "So big, all of you. Sally, what a young lady."

She giggled. "I danced at O-Bon, Dad. You should have seen me. Mrs. Watanabe said I was really good."

"Sakura!" Mom said, rolling her eyes at Dad.

He grinned. "I bet you were, Sally."

Mom took his arm and they began walking toward the cabin. Dad looked around. "These shacks—this is where we live?"

Mom nodded. "Yes. It is cramped. But wait till you see everything that Kenny did to make it better. Put up nails, organized our clothes . . ."

"And wait till you see the baseball field Kenny made," Mickey added. "He cleared it from nothing, Dad—"

"Kenny?" Dad sounded surprised. Kenny knew he was thinking, *Kenny did these things? Not Mickey?* Then he stopped walking and took Kenny by the arms. "Kenji," he said, his voice husky. "You look . . . different. So strong. So tall. So healthy."

"I am, Dad."

Dad looked at him for a long moment. They walked on.

Dad's face fell when he saw how small the shack was, and that it had no electricity, no running water, no toilet. But he commented on how comfortable and tidy the family had managed to make it, the shelf of jars over the woodstove, the neatly stacked firewood, the hooks and shelves, the space under the bed where the bedrolls were stored. And he laughed when Mom said,

"And you should see me use the woodstove, Harry. I'm a real pro."

"After a few disasters," Kenny teased.

Mom laughed, too. "Horrible, black disasters. But we managed. Kenny's kept us supplied with firewood, and hauled water every day—"

"Kenny, you shouldn't be hauling water!" Dad said, sounding alarmed.

"It's okay, Dad."

Again Dad gave him a long look.

"We'd better get over to the field," Mickey said. "The game was supposed to start already. The boys will be wondering where we are."

"The game?" Dad said.

As they walked over to the field, Mickey told Dad about all that Kenny had done. About clearing the field, organizing the boys, getting Mr. Richardson to pitch in, bringing baseball to the camp. Kenny felt his cheeks getting warmer and warmer. Dad didn't say anything, but every so often he glanced at him. There was a look of wonder on his face, as if he was recognizing his son and yet seeing him for the first time, all at once.

They arrived at the field. Some of the boys, in T-shirts

with a yellow sun or a red *N*, were tossing baseballs back and forth. Others, the lucky ones whose fathers had returned, were standing with their families, gesturing toward the field and talking in excited voices.

Kenny saw Tak with the fatherless boys. Tak glanced over, and a pained look crossed his face. Kenny waved. After a moment, Tak waved back.

Dad motioned from the backstop to the outfield, from the bases to the chalked base paths. "Kenny! You did this?"

"I didn't really, Dad. It was everybody, all together—"

"He did, Dad," Mickey said. "And that's not all." He swallowed. "He restored my honor."

"Your honor?" Dad said sharply. "What do you mean?"

Mickey reddened, but he didn't turn away. "I'll tell you another time, Dad. Not now. But believe me when I tell you that Kenny saved me. He brought me back."

Dad turned to Kenny. He put his hand on Kenny's shoulder. Kenny felt the warmth seep in.

Sammy ran over. "Mickey, all the boys are here. Can we start?"

"Sure, Sammy. Tell the teams to line up. We'll be there in a minute."

Sammy ran away. Kenny started to follow, but Mickey grabbed his arm. "Hold on, Kenny. I have something for you." He reached into his back pocket and pulled out his Asahi cap. He put it on Kenny's head.

Kenny reached up. "What? But—I'm not an Asahi."

"Don't worry, I'm not giving it to you," Mickey said with a laugh. "It's just for this game. But I want you to wear it."

Kenny's heart felt like it was swelling in his chest. *How many times have I dreamed of wearing this cap? But how can I? I'm not an Asahi.*

Dad lifted the brim of the cap where it had fallen over Kenny's forehead. He looked Kenny in the eye. "Kenny, I can't grasp what you have been doing here. It sounds"—he shook his head—"incredible. Miraculous. Later, you'll tell me. We have time, all the time in the world, and I want to hear everything. But for now, Mickey is right. You should wear this cap."

"But, Dad—"

Dad put his finger on Kenny's lips. He bent until he was at eye level with Kenny. "My son, I know you always wanted to be an Asahi—"

"You did?"

Dad smiled. "Yes, I did. And I know that you never had the chance. But, Kenny, it doesn't matter—because you have the heart of an Asahi. The heart of a champion."

He crushed Kenny to his chest. Then he looked at Kenny with the look that Kenny had never thought he'd see—the look he'd worn when Mickey had hit the winning run.

Kenny stood at home plate, facing Tak on the mound. The Asahi cap obscured his view, but he didn't care. There was no way he was taking it off.

His heart beat fast. His mouth was dry. His hands were sweaty.

Eye on the ball, he told himself. *Pivot and crouch. Shoulders square, knees loose.*

Breathe.

Tak reared back and threw. Kenny pivoted, squared off. He heard the sweet pop as the ball hit the bat. He felt the vibration. The ball sailed toward the shortstop. A perfect bunt.

Kenny dropped the bat and ran.

FURTHER READING

Adachi, Pat. *Asahi: A Legend in Baseball: A Legacy from the Japanese Canadian Baseball Team to its Heirs*, Coronex Printing and Publishing Ltd., 1992.

Aihoshi, Susan. *Torn Apart: The Internment Diary of Mary Kobayashi*, Scholastic Canada Ltd., 2012.

Furumoto, Ted Y. and Jackson, Douglas W. *More Than a Baseball Team: The Saga of the Vancouver Asahi*, Media Tectonics, 2012.

Hickman, Pamela and Fukawa, Masako. *Righting Canada's Wrongs: Japanese Canadian Internment in the Second World War*, Formac Lorimer Publishing, 2011.

Marcus, Jennifer. *Cherry Blossom Winter*, Dundern Press, 2012.

Pearce, Jacqueline. *The Reunion*, Orca Books, 2002.

Shimizu, Dr. Henry. *Images of Internment*, Ti-Jean Press, 2008.

Takashima, Shizuye. *A Child in Prison Camp*, Tundra Books, 1971.

WEBSITES

BC Sports Hall of Fame, http://www.bcsportshalloffame.com

The Canadian Baseball Hall of Fame and Museum, http://baseballhalloffame.ca

Virtual Museum of Canada, www.museevirtuel-virtualmuseum.ca